The Prose of the Mountains

OTHER TITLES IN THE SERIES

The Prose
of the
Mountains

Three Tales of the Caucasus

Aleksandre Qazbegi

Translated from the Georgian by Rebecca Gould

Central European University Press

Budapest ● New York

English translation © 2015 Rebecca Gould

Published in 2015 by

Central European University Press
An imprint of the
Central European University Limited Liability Company
Nádor utca 11, H-1051 Budapest, Hungary
Tel: +36-1-327-3138 or 327-3000
Fax: +36-1-327-3183
E-mail: ceupress@press.ceu.edu
Website: www.ceupress.com

224 West 57th Street, New York NY 10019, USA
Tel: +1-732-763-8816
E-mail: meszarosa@press.ceu.edu

The translation of the book has been funded by the Georgian National Book Center and the Ministry of Culture and Monument Protection of Georgia.

ISBN 978-6155053528
ISSN 1418-0162

Library of Congress Cataloging-in-Publication Data

Qazbegi, Alek'sandre, 1848-1893.
 [T'xzulebat'a sruli krebuli ot'x tomad, volume 1. English]
 The Prose of the mountains : three tales of the Caucasus / Aleksandre Qazbegi.
  pages cm -- (CEU Press classics)
 Translation based on the texts in following edition: T'xzulebat'a sruli krebuli ot'x tomad (Tbilisi: Gamomc'emloba "Sabchot'a Sak'art'velo", 1948-) Vol. 1.
 ISBN 978-6155053528 (pbk.)
 1. Qazbegi, Alek'sandre, 1848-1893--Translations into English. 2. Short stories, Georgian. I. Gould, Rebecca Ruth, translator. II. Qazbegi, Alek'sandre, 1848-1893. Eliso. English. III. Qazbegi, Alek'sandre, 1848-1893. Namcqemsaris mogonebani. English. IV. Qazbegi, Alek'sandre, 1848-1893. Khevis Beri Gocha. English. V. Title. VI. Title: Memoirs of a shepherd. VII. Title: Eliseo. VIII. Title: Khevis beri gocha.

PK9169.K3A2 2015
899'.969--dc23

2015004878

Contents

List of Illustrations

Note on Transliteration

As these translations are intended for an Anglophone audience, diacritics have been avoided. Hence, the capital city of Georgia is spelled as Tbilisi not the more orthographically correct T'bilisi. In the interest of preserving a one-to-one correspondence between the Georgian and English alphabets, both წ and ც have been transliterated by c (intended to be pronounced like ts as in hats). For the same reason, ხ is rendered by x rather than the more common kh. Distinctions between პ, ტ, თ and ო have not been reflected in this transliteration scheme.

Glossary

---

akaluxi—a thin garment made of cloth, including a shawl and a scarf.

beri—leader of the *temi* (s.v.), monk, elderly man (see *Xevi*).

bicho—literally, "boy." Used as a term of affectionate address in Georgian.

chinovnik—clerk (Russian).

chianuri—(also spelled *chunuri*) a three-stringed musical instrument, similar to a lute, with an oval body and a long neck. The national instrument of Svaneti, Racha, Guria, Xevsureti, and Tusheti. (The latter two regions border on Chechnya.) See figure 4.

choxa—the most typical clothing for a male mountaineer in the Caucasus. It covers the entire body like a thin cloak and reaches down to the feet. The ends are folded for more agile movement. The top part of a choxa consists of holes for storing bullets. See figure 2.

churchelo—a stalk of hardened pudding made of grape pulp, with sweetened walnuts in the middle, held together by a string.

Cminda Sameba—literally, "Holy Trinity," a historic church near the peak of Mt. Qazbeg (Mqinvari) and the town of Stephancminda (now Qazbegi), built in the fourteenth century. In addition to framing the scene for the site of "Xevisberi Gocha," Cminda Sameba was the subject of the Russian poet Pushkin's poem "Monastery on Kazbek" (1827). See figure 8.

Darial Gorge—a gorge on the border between Russia and Georgia, and hence a common dividing line between the north and south Caucasus. At various points in its history, the Darial Gorge has been controlled by Sasanians, the Rashidun Caliphate, the Kingdom of Georgia, Safavids, Qajars, and finally the Russian empire. For much of its length, it is bisected by the Terek (Tergi) River (s.v.). In the story "Eliso," this is the location of Vazhia's death. See figures 3 and 5.

Dzaug—the word used by Chechen and Georgian mountaineers for Vladikavkaz (s.v.).

Elbrus—the tallest mountain in the Caucasus; located on the Russian side of the Caucasus, but visible from Georgia.

giaour—a Muslim term for "unbeliever," also used by Georgian Christians to refer to themselves in contrast to Muslims. The Georgian is *giauri*. From Persian *gabr*, a Zoroastrian.

Imam Shamil (1797–1871)—a famous Daghestani Avar who fought against the Russians for twenty-four years (1835–1859). Shamil's Imamate united present-day Dagestan and Chechnya into a single political entity. He was highly respected across the Caucasus, including by Georgian writers such as Qazbegi.

Lars—(also Verkhnii Lars in Russian). A border crossing on the Georgian Military Road between Tbilisi and Vladikavkaz.

Lezgin—known as "Leki" in Georgian (Lezgin is the Russian ethnonym), the most populous ethnic group of Dagestan. They reside for the most part in southern Dagestan, near the Georgian border, and are famous for raiding Georgian territory.

Lomi—a Moxeve (s.v.) god still worshipped in the mountainous areas of northern Georgia with offerings of beer and prayers.

Marsha dooghiil—"Go freely" (Chechen).

Moxeve—a mountaineer from Xevi, the location of Stepancminda, adjoining the Darial Gorge.

Mqinvari—literally, "glacier," also called Mt. Qazbeg. One of the tallest mountains in the Caucasus, associated with the legend of Prometheus (Amirani) in Georgian folkore, who was chained to this mountain as punishment for stealing fire from the gods and giving it to humans. Located within the region of Xevi. See figures 1, 6, and 7.

Mtiuleti—a region bordering Xevi, in the mountains. The Mtiuletians are closely related to the Moxeves, Pshavs, and Tushetians, whereas Ossetians are considered an entirely separate ethnic and cultural group.

nabadi—a man's cloak made of wool, large enough to sleep inside; referred to as *burkha* in the north Caucasus (which is of course related to the Arabic *burqa'*, although the meaning is different).

nachalnik—overseer, administrator in the tsarist system (Russian).

naib—the Georgian spelling of "lieutenant, deputy, vice-regent" (Arabic, *nā'ib*). *Naibs* were the highest ranking officers in Imam Shamil's army.

Ossetian—an ethnic group that resides in the upper regions of Georgia and the north Caucasus in Russia. Considered by some Georgians to be a nonindigenous and not entirely trustworthy people.

panduri— four-stringed musical instrument, similar to a lute, with a circular body Similar to the *chianuri*, except it has one more string.

sazhen—Russian unit of measurement, equivalent to seven feet.

Sheni chirime—literally, "May your trouble be upon me," a polite form of address used in Georgian to indicate affection between two speakers. Roughly translatable as "My dear."

temi—1. a council of elders; 2. the collective voice of the community. The *temi* was the social structure around which every village in mountainous Georgia was organized, which resolved all internal and external disputes, filling in effect the function of a jury, and passing decisions concerning war. The leader of the *temi* was the *beri*.

Tergi River—the Georgian name for the river known as Terek in Russian, which was immortalized in the poems of Mikhail Lermontov.

tuman—currency in use in former Qajar territories everywhere in the Caucasus; anachronistically used in Georgian to denote Russian rubles.

verst—Russian unit for measuring length; the rough equivalent of two-thirds of a mile

Vladikavkaz—important trading center in the north Caucasus. Historically the home of the Ingush, it had by the time of Qazbegi's writing come to be more inhabited by Ossetians. In Russian, the name literally means "Rule the Caucasus," a clear sign of colonial designs. In Ingush and mountaineer Georgian, Vladikavkaz is called Dzaug or Dzaugi.

xabar—news, events, or stories (Arabic).

xevi—ravine, gorge, valley. Thus a *xevisberi*, such as Xevisberi Gocha, is a leader of a region built around a ravine.

Xevi—a small mountainous region of Georgia, where Cminda Sameba (Holy Trinity) church and Mt. Qazbeg (Georgian Mt. Mqinvari) are located.

Xevsur—mountaineer from Xevsureti, on Georgia's border with Chechnya.

Acknowledgments

I have acquired many debts over the years while working on these translations. First and foremost, I want to thank my talented and erudite teacher Tamriko Bakuradze, who introduced me to the Georgian language and read countless Georgian texts with me when I studied with her in Tbilisi. Tamriko is the best language teacher I ever had, not just in Georgian, but in any language. I hope that other aspiring Georgianists are blessed to work with her, and that her abilities in Georgian language pedagogy will continue to be recognized within and beyond Georgia.

Among other colleagues in the small field of Georgian Studies, I want to extend my gratitude to Paata Buxrashvili, Darejan Gardavadze, Paul Manning, Harsha Ram, Oliver Reisner, Donald Rayfield, Zaza Shatirishvili, and Kevin Tuite. Paul Manning in particular should be singled out for sharing his expertise on Georgian mountaineers, for his detailed and generous critiques, and for his kindness to me on all fronts. Outside Georgian Studies but still within Qazbegi's cultural sphere, I want to thank Robert Chandler for setting a high standard of translational excellence, John Colarusso for his wisdom and generous guidance, and Bruce Grant for his generosity towards me personally and professionally, and for his camaraderie during our conversations in Tbilisi, New York, Prague, and Philadelphia.

At Yale-NUS College, Regina Hong has been an extraordinary research assistant. I am grateful for her help with reviewing the proofs, and for her meticulous attention to detail.

Beth Gould provided much needed assistance at an early stage, and Kate Gould supported me in this and countless other endeavors.

Finally, I would like to thank my editor at Central European University Press, Szabolcs László, for his professionalism and dedication to this project.

Since this is my first book, and I was my mother's first child, I dedicate this translation to my mother, Brenda Gould.

Historical map of Georgia along the north Caucasus border, between the Caspian and the Black Sea (1872). Taken from Caucausus & Crimea with the Northern Portions of the Black & Caspian Seas, IX. (with) Crimea according to Huot & Demidoff. Drawn & Engraved by J. Bartholomew, Edinburgh. (with) The Caucasus according to Profr. Dr. Karl Koch, with additions from other Sources by Augustus Petermann, F.R.G.S. Engraved by G.H. Swanston. A. Fullarton & Co. London, Edinburgh & Dublin.

Qazbegi: A Biographical Note[1]

Like the Georgian writers who preceded him, Qazbegi was a member of the aristocracy. His family had replaced their original surname, Chopikashvili, with the name of their feudal title, *qazbegi*, which eventually also became the name of his village (more commonly known as Stepancminda during his lifetime) and the nearby mountain (more commonly known as Mqinvari). Instead of enjoying the life his high birth could have afforded him, he chose a life of deliberate poverty, first in Stepancminda, a small mountain village near the place of his birth, where he lived as a shepherd for seven years, and subsequently in Tbilisi. While busy crafting a fresh literary style for a new readerly demographic, Qazbegi soon emerged as Georgia's first professional writer. He died at the age of forty-five in an insane asylum in Tbilisi. The cause of his death is unknown, as are the reasons for his institutionalization; it is generally believed that he had contracted syphilis. After his death, Qazbegi was

---

[1] For a fuller discussion of Qazbegi's style, and an attempt to situate his works in the Georgian literary tradition, see the Afterword to this volume.

buried in Stepancminda. During the Soviet period, Qazbegi's home was turned into a museum, and his stature towers over Stepancminda to this day.

Qazbegi's first literary influences were Maupassant, from whom he learned to structure short stories, and Dostoevsky, whose work he encountered during his student days in St. Petersburg, and from whom he learned how to create narrative tension through dialogue. Although he was immersed in Russian and French narrative prose, Qazbegi crafted from these European influences an anticolonial perspective that was missing from the traditions preceding him. He also introduced new perspectives on mountaineer life into the Georgian literary canon. In his life and his writing, at times with subtlety and at other times caustically, Qazbegi critiqued the many Georgian poets who aligned their literary vocations with imperial rule and who, in his view, were too willing to surrender Georgia's political autonomy to the armies of the tsar.

That Georgian prose fiction begins with Qazbegi was recognized by the poet Grigol Orbeliani (1804–1888), who belonged to the class of colonial officials toward whom Qazbegi directed his sharpest critiques. After reading Qazbegi's *Elguja* (1881), a novel offering an unprecedented critique of Russian colonial politics and its impact on Georgian society, Orbeliani called this rising star "Georgian literature's new Homer."

For Qazbegi, prose fiction was a means of speaking truth to power, of saying things that other forms and genres, including poetry, could not say. Through empathetic characterizations of Chechens, Ingush, and Georgian mountaineers such as the Moxeves and Xevsurs, and through historical narratives that ranged from the sixteenth to the nineteenth century, Qazbegi envisioned a Caucasus that recognized the plurality of cultures, literatures, and belief systems that most richly constitute this region's history, and that are all too frequently eclipsed by more easily assimilable political norms.

Fig. 1. Mount Qazbeg (Mqinvari) in snow

Memoirs of a Shepherd

I

In 18— I decided to become a shepherd. I was prepared to traverse hills and fields in pursuit of this trade. I wanted to know the lives of the people, to experience from within the pleasures and fears suffusing their lives. Being a mountaineer, I had a few sheep already. I had received other sheep in exchange for some plots of land. So I picked up a stick and my gun and became a shepherd.

Everyone regarded my decision as a joke. They said that the son of a respected nobleman had no business being a shepherd. But I had my reasons for the path I had chosen. My desire to become a shepherd was so powerful that I was deaf to all advice. I wanted to see these people. I wanted to experience their yearnings. I wanted to live their lives and to bear witness to the trials and tribulations that punctuate the lives of shepherds and that they kept hidden in their souls.

I achieved my goal. I came to know intimately those shepherds whom I was ready to give my life to live with. How I learned of their lives is the subject of the following pages.

It was still summer. The rams were wet and the ewes had not yet been milked. Two Moxeves appeared in the road who had never seen me before. From the way I was dressed, they couldn't make out whether I was a simple shepherd or the son of a respected nobleman.

"May your flocks multiply!" they yelled once they were within hearing range.

"May God multiply your happiness!" I responded.

"Child, whose sheep are those?" they asked.

I answered with my last name, not mentioning that the name belonged to me as well as to the owner of the sheep.

"Well, I'll be damned, they really do bear that mark. No one else has a seal like that," the first Moxeve said and then asked, "Who is your father?"

"I am Arakhvetili, my friends," I answered in the Mtiuleti dialect. "Burlian Iakobani is my father."

"Are you a hired worker or do you share these sheep with other shepherds?" they asked.

"I share these sheep, my friends," I answered.

The Moxeves stood by my side and helped me call the sheep back from their pasture.

"What is your name, child?"

"Mamuka, my friends."

"Does the son of a lord really run with the sheep?"

"Yes, he does indeed run with the sheep, by the grace of Lomisi," I answered.

"So now lords run around in the fields?" they asked in surprised unison.

"Yes, indeed," I said.

"By God, that's odd!"

"Why do you say that?" I asked. My heart began to palpitate and I pricked up my ears.

"You see nothing strange in the son of a lord chasing after sheep?" They waved their hands.

"What's so strange about that?" I asked. "I have sheep and I prefer to pasture them by myself."

"Strange?" The first speaker said. "The son of a lord of Xevi and a simple shepherd at the same time? You don't see anything strange about that?"

"Your ancestors had sheep, too," answered the second Moxeve. "They didn't look after them on their own, thank God! But they would never think of being shepherds themselves, thank God."

"Just look how low we have sunk in this corrupt age!" the first Moxeve said.

"Things have changed since then," I said, attempting to justify myself.

"Whether or not that's true, you must be good-for-nothing. If you hadn't concocted this grand scheme of becoming a shepherd, then you could have become the governor of Kvesh."

These words pained me so much that I couldn't continue speaking. The sheep were running in circles around me, anxious for grazing. I took them to the mountain where they ran back and forth; it was still too early in the day for milking. The strangers bid me farewell and left me alone, newly saddened by society's judgment against me and absorbed in my thoughts.

The mist lifted and fresh dew seeped from the sky. I put on my shawl and hat and stood in front of my sheep to keep track of those who were ahead of the rest. They were running on an empty stomach and I didn't want them to lose their appetite. Not much time passed before I noticed two bearded men in formal clothing making their way toward me. I stared at them in surprise; if they were merely travelers, then they should have been approaching from the opposite direction.

My dog, Basara, rushed toward them with a bark. They took hold of their sticks, but I called to him to stay calm. Basara wagged his tail and ran back toward me. The strangers smiled and mumbled in broken Russian: "Dog, dog. No bite."[2]

"No bite," I answered in equally broken Russian.

"Sheep, sheep," one of the foreigners began. He couldn't finish his sentence in Russian, so he turned to his companion and asked in French: "How do I ask, 'Where is wool sold?'"

"I don't know either," the second companion answered in French.

They continued talking about wool and expressed surprise that such a large flock of sheep could be housed in the mountains. They started musing on how much wool I sold and how many sacks of wool I could collect.

I understood everything they said because I knew French quite well. Unable to restrain myself any longer, I interrupted: "There are many sheep in the mountains! People almost live with sheep, we have so many. Even Armenian merchants come here to buy our wool."

Imagine their shock, when in those strange, wild mountains, inhabited, so the foreigners imagined, only

---

[2] The text here is given in Russian.

by barbarians who didn't know how to count past ten, all of a sudden a simple shepherd appeared who not only could understand French but could even speak the language fluently.

"What!" They exclaimed together. "You speak French?"

"Yes, a little."

"Amazing! Where did you study French?"

I was in the mood to enjoy myself. So I answered, "All shepherds in this region speak French. I've worked in other places, and so my French is rusty, but, as for the other shepherds, you wouldn't be able to distinguish their French from the French of a native speaker."

"Amazing! This is a curious business!" they said to each other. "We thought you were barbarians!"

We talked for a while longer, until they grew tired. I became bored by their nonsense. They asked me for directions to Qazbegi station, where they intended to spend the night. Before leaving, they asked me to tell them about the lives, customs, and character of the Georgian people. At last, they asked me: "Have you heard of England and France?"

"Yes," I answered, nodding my head.

"He is from France and I am from England," one of them said to me and added, "We will write in our books everything you have told us when we return to our countries, then everyone will read these books. Come home with us. We will give you money."

"Thank you," I said. "I will go home with you."

The Frenchman slipped his hand into his pocket, took out some rubles and stretched out his hand, beckoning me to take them. "Keep this money until this evening," he said. "Tonight we will give you even more."

"Thank you," I said, turning red with embarrassment. "I'll meet you tonight and you can give all the money to me then."

"Take the money, don't be shy."

"I'll take it this evening, sir."

"As you wish, then. Let it be this evening," he answered. The foreigners bid me farewell, and I directed my sheep toward my village and then sent them to pasture.

A fellow shepherd came down to help me that evening. He had returned from the mountain on which he had nourished a ewe back to the milking stage. A young boy accompanied him, to help us guard the sheep.

"Come in peace," I greeted them as they arrived.

"May God grant you peace," they answered.

"How are your sheep?" I asked them.

"Not bad. I bring my lambs every day to Qirvan and they play there. What else can I tell you? They're well-fed and satisfied."

"How are the lands for pasturing?"

"There's not much to say. My cucumbers are round—" here my friend broke off. "But I came to see you on other business," he resumed. "The Mistress asked me to tell you to come down from the mountains for a few minutes. Guests have come to see you."

"Who are they?"

"How should I know who they are? They came from the city. Some kind of officers, I think."

"Are there women with them?"

"Yes, there are women."

"Then I'll go, but I'm counting on you. Pay attention to the sheep. Don't let any of them get away."

"Don't be afraid. Nothing bad will happen to them."

I said goodbye and pet my loyal dog, who had grown so accustomed to my sheep that he couldn't stand being separated from them, and set off for home.

It was a splendid moonlit evening. My guests were coming out of the garden, drinking their tea. From their joyful laughter and manner of speaking I deduced that they must have been enjoying themselves. I started walking in their direction. After a few steps, I noticed a relative of mine among the group whom I had not seen for ages. I hurried to meet him. The old man accompanying him happened to be one of my father's closest friends. I had intended to change my clothes before greeting him, but the guests caught sight of me and called to me to come over to them. I asked their pardon for my dirty clothes and went to see them. I felt quite awkward to have my relative see me dressed like this. But imagine my surprise when, as soon as I arrived, the old man greeted me with the following words:

"Lord almighty! Look at this child of the lord of this mountain! For shame!"

I stood frozen with my hand outstretched to shake the hand of the relative I had not seen in so many years, while the old man simply stared at me with stupefaction. My young relations stood to the side and chuckled to themselves.

"Aren't you ashamed of yourself? Don't you have a conscience?" the angry old man asked me.

"Why are you attacking me, my good man?" I barely managed to articulate. "What crime have I committed?"

"How can you even ask such a question?" The old man yelled at me. "Young man, did your father raise you to be a shepherd? Did he waste all his savings on your education so you would turn out like this? If all you wanted was to live like a shepherd, you son of a bitch, then why did you go to Russia? Why did you waste so much money on your education? I could have given you to my own shepherd. He could have taught you how to be a shepherd better than anyone else!"

"My father lived as he pleased, and I intend to live according to my wishes as well," I said. My insides were on fire.

"He went to the *people*. He wanted to experience the lives of the low classes, the prince!" said one of the young officers, smiling.[3]

"Whether I want to live like the people or not is none of your business!" I yelled. "But I will tell you one thing. I'll take being a shepherd any day over shooting the breeze like you. At least shepherds do something useful."

---

[3] The speakers are referencing the activities that were associated with the *narodniks*, a group of Russian intellectuals who practiced a philosophy of going back to "the people [*narod*]." Georgia had its own version of the *narodniks*, called the *xalxosnebi*, but Qazbegi was not among them. For this movement, see inter alia Oliver Reisner, *Die Schule der georgischen Nation: eine sozialhistorische Untersuchung der nationalen Bewegung in Georgien am Beispiel der "Gesellschaft zur Verbreitung der Lese- und Schreibkunde unter den Georgiern"* (1850–1917) (Wiesbaden: Reichert, 2004).

I turned and set off toward the house. When I reached my room I heard the enraged old man shout some nonsensical phrase and the young people laughing at his words. Then the old man cried: "Why do you want to get close to the people? What is the point? You say that today's generation is useless and good for nothing. It will never create anything worthwhile."

The officer was outraged by this idea and interrupted the old man's speech: "What on earth is the meaning of this? Why do you try to force everyone to think like you? Our relative only became a shepherd because he wanted to show off. Surely, not everyone is as silly as he is!"

"There's nothing special about being a shepherd. What do I have to show off?"

Those were the last words I ever heard from my guests. I shut the door and their voices vanished from my consciousness. On the one hand, they blamed me because I refused the silver-lined path that had been chiseled out for me before my birth. I was to blame for not pursuing the glory and the rank that would cast honor on their name. On the other hand, they berated me because, instead of incessantly lamenting the meaninglessness of my life and the parasitism of my class, I took up a challenging profession that actually had fulfilled a useful purpose. Among the shepherds, I was plagued by their distrust, because those sincere people, whom I strove with all my heart to befriend, couldn't imagine a man from the aristocracy who didn't want to rob them, and instead dreamed of working with them in fraternity and friendship.

Such was the debut of my career as a shepherd on the stage of life. I passed seven years of my life pursuing this craft. In the following pages you, dear reader, will see what I saw, felt, and understood during these seven years.

II

Autumn arrived. The other shepherds noticed that I passed the entire summer with the animals. I had no shelter or roof above my head, so, like most of them, I waited. I didn't melt like sugar. I didn't get bored or sick, although God knows how many times the rain poured over my head. Gradually, everyone understood that I could not easily be dissuaded from the mission I had undertaken, that I would not abandon my path without having achieved my goal.

During this time I made friends with many shepherds, but most of all with one shepherd from Stepancminda named Svimon Gigaur. Svimon impressed me with his intelligence and quick wit upon our first meeting. He was the exact prototype of a shepherd from the mountains; thoughtful and sensitive, afraid of hurting even a worm. But, whenever he saw injustice, he dedicated all his strength to fighting it. He was attractive, well-built, and had a reputation for fairness. Everyone loved him, especially his singing. He was famous throughout Xevi for his experience and skill in tending to the sheep.

III

Some time passed as I prepared the paperwork for the border crossing. Across from Stepancminda, on the banks of the Tergi River, all the shepherds were gathered together, dressed in black. We called to each others' sheep, because we planned to leave the next day. In keeping with tradition, we scheduled the trip for evening.

The shepherds parted from their friends and relatives with such drama that it seemed as though they were going to war, or expecting disaster. The Nakh and Chechens of the plains differ in important ways from us. But they are peaceful people, just like us. Why are these hardworking people so feared when they go about their business peacefully? I was still innocent at the time these reflections occurred to me, and everything appeared strange. I had no idea of all the pain and suffering awaiting us in our journey across the mountains.

The shepherds selected me as their leader. Svimon was chosen as my assistant. During the feasts, the shepherds brought me cup after cup of whatever liquid I pleased, and even composed poems in my honor, with all the desires and hopes they had projected onto me.

The sun was already descending beyond the horizon by the time we finished our meal. I made ready to fulfill my duties. The shepherds were so pessimistic about the clashes awaiting us that I felt it was necessary to make sure we were well-armed. I called our shepherds to assemble and surveyed those who possessed weapons. Their pistols were beautifully polished, their swords sharpened, and we possessed an ample store of gunpowder and bullets. I was content. We were ready for battle, at whatever moment it might arrive.

The sheep were supposed to stay that evening and leave the next morning at the crack of dawn for the Cossack station near Makhan-Yurt, where we had reserved a place for them for the winter. Svimon and I went to the village to take care of the remaining business and to put things in order.

"These are elaborate preparations, Svimon," I said, "I don't understand what it's all for."

"Better now than when it's too late," he said cryptically.

"You talk as though we were preparing for war!" I wished he would explain to me what kind of danger was awaiting us.

"What difference does it make whether a man who goes to battle is a soldier or a shepherd? Either way, they won't get very far without weapons."

"How's that?"

"It's like this," Svimon said. "Everything threatens sheep: predators, men, weather, what have you. Everything is the enemy of sheep. That's why a shepherd is the unhappiest of all men. Any artisan or common worker can put his work off for another time if he doesn't feel like working. But a shepherd must work regardless of the weather or whatever pain may be haunting him. When anyone else would stay at home, the shepherd must protect his flock. Even during the night, he can't close his eyes, for fear that a wolf or thief will spy his flock. There's no rest for him, day or night."

Svimon spoke the truth. Imagine a shepherd beneath the dark, cold, naked sky. There is nowhere to hide from the incessant rain pouring from the sky like water from a bucket, and the shepherd is doused to the very threads of his clothing, as the marrow of his bones freeze solid and the wind tears away his cloak as the coldness prickles his skin. It is impossible for him to seek shelter because he must tend to his flock.

At daybreak we set off again on our journey, after paying homage to our ancestors and the holy saints of Xevi.

We divided our flock into five parts. Svimon walked in front and I stayed at the rear of the procession. I insisted upon this sequence in spite of the fact that he wanted me in front.

As we were walking I made my mind that no matter what would happen in the future, there would come a time when I would have to violate the general will and interfere in their affairs when they did not wish me to. Only in that way would it be possible for me to protect the flock and to come to their assistance when necessary.

Our flock reached a winding path, and we walked after it at a slow gait. Finally, we reached the Darial Gorge. The first fifth of the flock came to a sudden halt. A scream resounded from somewhere not far away. Soon, a shepherd arrived with the news that the Cossacks had refused us permission to cross the Darial. There was indeed a special station at the Darial for Cossacks to review the paperwork of shepherds on their way to winter pastures.

"Why have they stopped us?" I asked.

"Because they want to torment us," the shepherd said as though the reason were obvious.

I hurried to the post and saw the Cossacks herding the sheep into a wagon filled with dirt. Our newly washed sheep were putrefied to their knees. The Cossacks were shoving the sheep into the wagon without distinguishing between male and female. There was a risk that some of the ewes would be impregnated too early and would give birth when there was no grass for grazing in the pastures. Their nipples would be barren during this season. The soft lambs would have no nourishment, and perhaps would perish altogether. Their legs would be sore after standing for so long in the dirt. It would be impossible to send them to pasture without endangering their lives. They would not be able to clear away the snow and feed on the grass buried beneath the frost. Even if they lived through winter, they would be so emaciated after all they had endured that they would not yield any wool or milk.

Of course, the local Cossacks had long been used to making their living from stealing. They possessed no conscience or sense of shame, nor any grasp of the suffering they inflicted as they detained the shepherds. Even with all my experience with the ways of the Cossacks, I was surprised by the brutality they displayed in their dealings with us this time.

As soon as I arrived, I was surrounded with my own and foreign shepherds.

"Save us!" They cried. "Save us, in the name of St. Giorgi!"

"What's disturbing them?" I asked. "Why aren't they allowed to cross the border?"

"The Cossacks insist that we pay them *tumans*," a merchant informed me. "If they can't come up with the money, then they won't be allowed to cross the border."

"We offered to pay one *tuman*, but the Cossacks wouldn't accept it," added another merchant.

"Why should you pay anything at all?" I broke out in a rage and turned to a Cossack standing nearby. "Who's the eldest among you?" I asked.

"And why would you want to know?" he shot back.

"Are you the *nachalnik*?" I asked again.

"Yes, I'm the *nachalnik*. What's it to you?" he sneered.

"Why aren't you allowing this flock to pass?" I asked.

"I don't want them to pass, and therefore I don't allow it," he said.

"Do you know how much the shepherds are losing over this delay?"

"What business is that of mine?" the leader said.

I finally understood that there was no point in trying to negotiate with this man. He was a liar passing himself off as the leader of the Cossacks. Nowhere did his clothes bear the mark of any official rank.

I went silently to the barracks. Another Cossack met me at the entrance.

"Where are you headed?" he stopped me.

"I want to see your *nachalnik*."

"He's busy drinking, and has no time to see you."

"Go and tell him that I must speak with him." I gave my first and last name.

"Just who do you think you are? Our *nachalnik*?" the Cossack laughed.

I was barely able to control my rage.

The supervisor was indeed deeply immersed in drink, and when I approached him, everyone burst into laughter. What was I to do? It worked in my favor that I spoke fluent Russian. If someone else had been in my position without knowing Russian he would have had to listen to even worse insults.

I returned to the shepherds and told them to remove their sheep from the wagons and hurry onward. My unhappy comrades broke the gates and released their imprisoned sheep. The sheep jumped eagerly from their wagons into freedom.

One of the Cossacks ran up to us and hit a shepherd with his whip. The shepherd turned and lunged at the Cossack, who was trying to escape. He hurled the Cossack to the ground and was about to attack him further until I managed to intervene. But the shouts of the Cossack had reached his companions, and soon a battle was underway. There was no contest in the clash between ten Cossacks and eighty of Xevi's best shepherds.

Soon the Cossacks were begging for an end to the fighting. They called their *nachalnik*, a drunken fellow named Belogorov or Belogorsky, I don't remember which. He appeared in a nightshirt, drunk and barely able to stand up straight.

"Weapons!" he shouted, as soon as he saw the battle.

Once he realized that his army was on the brink of defeat, he hurried back into the barracks, put on a *choxa* and a ritual sword and bowed before me obsequiously.

It was only with great difficulty that I managed to calm down the shepherds. We escorted our flock back onto the road, and, to the great joy of my comrades, continued on our journey.

Fig. 2. *Georgian Man in a Choxa*, from Arthur Leist, *Das Georgische Volk* (Dresden: E. Pierson's Verlag, 1903), 233.

IV

Barely had we recovered from our clash with the Darial Cossacks, when another group of Cossacks from Lars crossed our path, demanding a fine for every lamb in the flock. Why and for what end the money was to be used—these details remained a mystery. They continued to insist, and we continued to refuse. It seemed that another fight was inevitable. May God bless the local observer who informed the authorities that I was in charge of the shepherds. This saved us from another battle. The shepherds rejoiced at their unexpected fortune.

Before we had traveled much further, we spied a line of bonfires on the Chalka River. These fires were stocked by our hosts, now preparing dinner.

We decided to sleep as soon as we arrived by the fires. We set the sheep to pasture; they had to replenish themselves after a long day roaming along the endless paths of the gorge. If any grass had been growing along the paths, it had been trampled long before by the flocks that preceded them.

"Just look at them!" Svimon yelled as he approached me.

"What are you afraid of?" I asked. "Are there Cossacks?"

"Wolves gather, just like Ossetians congregate."

"What do you mean?"

"Come and see for yourself. There's no relief from the Ossetians."

"What are you talking about?"

"They brought bottles of vodka to us as though they planned to treat us, but they were really spying, trying to see how they could best steal our flock."

"What are you saying? That's impossible."

"You have strength. Your father is the equal in power to the tsar. Maybe they don't laugh in front of you, but when you aren't there, you have no idea what goes on."

"So what are we to do?"

"They've already found out." Svimon cut himself short and stuffed a rock into the mouth of a sheep who was incessantly chewing on something.

"There's enough land to go around for everyone. Why can't those cursed bastards understand that?"

We didn't speak for much longer. I went to inspect the place we had reserved for the night. I was surprised by how sturdily it had been fortified. It seemed as though the shepherds were expecting not to sleep but to do battle. Our escort was busy clearing the ground. When he saw me, he waved enthusiastically, radiating the aura of someone ready to fight. He had been entrusted with a sacred task and was determined to carry it out honorably. In addition to that, he deemed it his duty to bow before me as to an elder.

Our campsite was encircled by hills, the tops of which provided beautiful views of the surroundings. The site itself resembled a field covered with moist grass, from which a river flowed.

"You chose well," I said, "except that the forest's rather far from us." I struggled for more to say.

"We need to stay as far as possible from the forest."

"Why?"

"If a wolf or thief plan to steal our sheep, they won't be able to do it, so long as they're protected by our campsite," he explained as he straightened his hat. "I'm a mountaineer and a shepherd. I know how to handle these things."

There was nothing left for me to say, so we walked over silently to the bonfire. Even from far away I could see that the fire was set up to warm more people than had come to tend the flock, and I recalled Svimon's warning.

"This is set up for many people," I said to my companion. "Why is that?"

"It's for the Ossetians, so they'll think we're a large group and stay away! Whoever sees this bonfire won't dare to approach us."

When I arrived at the bonfire, a group of Ossetians jumped to their feet and bowed deeply before me. They declared the devotion they owed me because my father had been unreservedly generous with them. They wished to honor his memory, they explained, and ended with the following:

"Whenever Glaxa's flock"—Glaxa was my father's name—"crossed our path he always gave us a ram."

One of the Ossetians told of how my father had given him a ram the size of an elephant and an ox almost as big as well. Then they brought out a bottle of vodka and insisted that I drink with them in front of the fire. There was no end of their singing. One of the shepherds departed to find a lamb. That provided an excuse for me to leave as well. I only managed to extricate myself with difficulty; the Ossetians keep insisting that they be appointed to watch over our flock during the night.

"You're our guest, *sheni chirime*, and we're your host. Let us treat you as a host is supposed to treat his guest."

The shepherds frowned so intensely that I was afraid to take the Ossetians up on their offer. Finally, I was free from my self-appointed hosts. The night had arrived and with it came the time for the guards to exchange places. The new guards gathered some food and left with their sheep dogs to the borders of the campsite to protect our flock.

We assembled around the fire to devour the steaming hot cornmeal dumplings that made up the majority of our food supply. The shepherds laughed and joked after lunch, improvising poems for each other. I delighted in being near these good-hearted people who seemed to have not a care in the world. A stern fate had curbed their chances in life, but in spite of all they had endured, their faces glowed with radiance.

They slowly smoked on their pipes as they unrolled their *nabadis* to rest. Even though they looked forward to a long night of talking and work, they had to get some sleep.

The moon hid behind the mountains. The darkness became thick as fog, and the stars glowed more brilliantly. Every object and person in the vicinity basked in the silence of their light. The paths with all their passersby disappeared from the mountains. The peaks seemed to rise from the ground and then to disappear in the clouds. The Tergi whispered not far away, recalling a long-forgotten lullaby. No wolves could be seen or heard, because the sheep dogs were calmly guarding the flock.

The smell of freshly cut hay and flowers saturated the air of this astonishingly silent night. These aromas created a feeling of life in anyone who happened to be close enough to imbibe their scent. Life seemed to be a

21

force full of sweetness and love. It seemed as though anything was possible and everything a joy. At least that's how it seemed to me, and that's how I believe it seemed to everyone else on the mountain.

I don't know about my companions, but I wasn't able to fall asleep. A thousand thoughts rocked back and forth in my mind. They carried me to realms unseen and I found it impossible to release myself from them.

A great deal of time passed as I became drunk on the scents of the hay and the flowers and my eyelids began to feel heavy. I was falling asleep when a shriek interrupted the silence. The shriek was followed by a crossfire of bullets and shepherds' cries.

I jumped to my feet. My companions were already wide awake and ready for action. They hurriedly gathered the flock together. The sheep ran with their heads to the ground. It was so dark that they couldn't make out the path in front of them. Near the bonfire, the shepherd dogs fought with the wolves. A second later, one wolf fell to the ground. The dogs attacked him and tore him to pieces.

The shepherds finally managed to gather together and calm down the entire flock. The sheep continued running back and forth until they stumbled over some rock or other object lodged in the ground, or until they were overcome with dizziness and collapsed on their feet.

As dawn broke through the horizon, I wondered to myself, "Has another day of incessant work and no rest arrived? What future awaits us? When will I be able to sleep?"

V

Light filled the air. Shouts and whistles circulated among the shepherds. The flock hurried forward along the path. We had not had a chance to enter the Balt Forest when we were detained by border guards demanding payment for a fine. It seemed that they expected us to pay them for the right to walk on the earth. Our sheep had been walking over the fields, not the roads, in order to graze on the grass, we explained. However, no one was listening to our protests. We had to submit. We handed our documents, in which were recorded the size of our flock and other livestock, to the offenders. They didn't even so much as glance as our documents. Instead they insisted on counting all over again the number of our sheep.

Just imagine how long it took to count eight thousand sheep! Just imagine how much we wanted to interrupt their pointless maneuverings against us!

I tried to convince the *nachalnik* to accept the figures recorded on our paperwork, but all in vain.

"We are required to count them," he repeated flatly. It seemed that these were the only words in his vocabulary.

The flock assembled on the road and chaos ensued. Neither carts nor coaches nor camels nor any other vehicle was allowed to pass as they blocked the thoroughfare. Everything came to a standstill.

I decided to guide our flock over to a small field, not far from the Balt Forest, and to keep them stationed there until we were on our way to Vladikavkaz. It was all

23

of twelve versts from Balt to Vladikavkaz. I was longing to meet Monsieur Delacroix, the French official in charge of these roads. We were good friends, and he would have wanted to be informed of all the anarchy reigning over his dominions.

As soon as I approached the *nachalnik* with the intention of informing him of my plans, a man dressed in an officer's uniform hurried up to me.

"You're getting angry over nothing," he told me.

"What do you mean, over nothing?" I asked in surprise, and added, "We haven't used your roads. We didn't destroy anything of yours or anyone else's. You have no right to demand money from us. But of course the word 'right' means nothing to you. You don't trust the documents issued by your own officers and stamped with a government seal. Instead you insist on counting everything from scratch, in spite of what it costs us to wait."

"There's one law for everyone. That's the order of our *nachalnik*."

"I find it hard to believe that your *nachalnik* ordered you: 'Torture these people and do harm to them in whatever way you can.'"

"You're getting angry over nothing," he repeated. He was clearly just an innocent boy from the village. This was clear from the clothes he wore and the expression on his face.

My interlocutor was cleanly dressed. His face was pale, his hat was straight, and his hair was doused in pig fat. His appearance simultaneously betokened cleverness and guile. He was a cross between a donkey and a demon. The furls of his mustache gleamed from pomade. Upstart country bumpkins like him decorate their speeches with excess words when their supply runs low and carelessly utter whatever comes into their head. In a word, my interlocutor belonged to that class of people with whom it's impossible to carry on a decent conversation.

"What do you mean by saying it's over nothing?" I insisted, getting angrier with every moment that passed.

"All you have to do is give the officers three or four lambs and they'll let you go," he explained.

"Not only will we not give them three lambs," I said. "We won't give them three hairs of sheepskin!"

"As you wish," he replied, "but it would be easier for everyone if you would cooperate." He rolled a cigarette and offered it to me. "Will this calm you down?"

"I thank you," I said and ordered a shepherd standing nearby to bring my horse.

"So you're planning to leave?" he asked me.

"Yes, I need to go straightaway to Mr. Delacroix and inform him of the behavior of your colleagues."

"If you ask me—"

"You have nothing to say on the matter," I interrupted him. All my patience had evaporated.

The shepherd brought my horse. I barely managed to put my feet into the stirrups, when the soldier approached me again.

"Why don't you just give me two lambs?" he said. "They'll stop counting and let you go, I promise."

"Just listen to yourself! Some passerby is promising a peaceful citizen protection in exchange for two lambs!

First they take his documents. Then they interrupt everyone's journey along their roads. Then they demand
compensation!" I continued thinking to myself, "What
has happened to this world?"

"Why don't we just give them one of our dogs?"
Svimon suggested. "Then they'll let us go."

"Never!" I shouted. "This time at least we'll teach
these thieves how to behave."

Svimon laughed, "That will only work if they're capable of learning."

"If we make them learn, then they'll learn."

"Isn't their chief a man by the name of Qipiani? By
the time we return, another will be in his place, and he
will do the same thing as Qipiani is doing now."

"Just listen to you talk!" I said in irritation. "You'd
think that every single person on earth is a thief."

"That's not what I'm saying. Just that there's a great
deal of injustice in the world. But since you're insisting:
let's try crossing the river. That way we can avoid using
their road."

"What are you talking about, *bicho*!" another shepherd
interrupted our conversation. "Last year we passed
through both Zde and Jariaxi and we made it all the way
to Dzaug without once being stopped by anyone. But
then the Cossacks chased us and forced us to pay even
more than they usually do."

"That's impossible!" I exclaimed. "You made it past
the state road and only then you were forced to pay the
road patrol?"

"Yes, indeed, I swear by the mercy of the Spars angels!"

I didn't believe him at the time. Only later, having seen several such incidents myself, did I realize that he was telling the truth.

I wanted to do as Svimon advised, if only to find out from experience whether we would be exposed to such illegality. But as it turned out, the bridge that had been built by the residents themselves had been designed by a local engineer, and the water was too deep to ford by a boat. So I decided that no matter what I would make it to Vladikavkaz. But, as if to spite me, at precisely this moment, a carriage pulled up in front of us, and Mr. Delacroix stepped out. I approached him and informed him of our troubles. He reproached the *nachalnik* for misbehaving and told him, "You must remember who you have business with. You cannot act the same with everyone."

I was asking for justice, not privileges. So I interrupted Mr. Delacroix.

"Dear Sir, I was asking not for privileges or special dispensations, but simply for my rights as a citizen under the law."

"You're a strange man!" Mr. Delacroix responded. "We can't treat you as though you were a simple peasant!"

"In this situation," I said, "whether I am a peasant or a nobleman is irrelevant. We're all the same under the law."

"That may be true in theory," Mr. Delacroix responded, "but it will never be true in fact." He shook his head.

We continued speaking a great deal longer. The business ended with our not being charged anything, in spite of the fact that I demanded that the *nachalnik* apply to me the same regulations as would be applied to anyone else.

Soon we arrived in Vladikavkaz and set our flock loose to graze the field. Now we had to get permission from those who were renting the fields that belonged to the city of Vladikavkaz.

VI

Wide fields opened before our eyes as we approached the city. White smoke ascended from the edges of the fields. This was the city of Dzaug, which had been changed by the Russians into Vladikavkaz.

After a difficult two-week journey, the sheep consumed the grass greedily, as though afraid it would soon be gone. The shepherds finally breathed freely. They knew that troubles still awaited us after Dzaug, but shepherds from the mountains are like steel. They knew they would be able to overcome all obstacles.

Powerful waters flowed over the open plains, through the deserted forest, beneath the rushing Tergi. The waves raced forward, foaming into their heights and flowing quickly into your imagination. When viewing sights like this, it seems that nature herself is telling you what to do.

Some riders crossed our path when we drew closer to Vladikavkaz.

"Whose flock is that?" one rider asked.

"Ours," the shepherds answered in unison.

"Who is the eldest among you?"

One of the shepherds pointed at me and said, "He's the eldest."

The riders informed me that we had to compensate them in both money and sheep for the use of their fields. They also wanted to know how long we planned to remain in the region.

We had planned to stay in Vladikavkaz for at least three days. We had to prepare for an eight-month stay in the mountains, to purchase clothing and other provisions, to sell our rams, and to set our business affairs in order.

One of the riders handed me a piece of paper. "This is so you won't forget the day of your departure," he explained. "We are the city guards."

I took the paper and began to read it. Imagine my surprise: it was claimed that we had arrived on the first of September when the actual date was the sixth.

"You made a mistake," I said. "Today's the sixth. Here you have written the first of the month."

"Show me," one of the riders instructed. "What difference is it to you?" he then whispered in my ear. "Don't disagree with us. You'll get your reward either way."

At first I didn't understand what he meant by "reward." Then it dawned on me: the conversation was about money. So in Vladikavkaz, as everywhere, the officials lived on bribes and theft, taking for their victims simple shepherds.

In order to understand just how this larceny took place, it is necessary to remember that the mountaineers don't know Russian. When they cross the fields during winter there are many occasions for transacting business with local officials who know only Russian. The shepherds may be accompanied by a translator who knows Russian, but often the only person they can find is someone whose Russian is barely passable, who spends all his time trying to please the tsarist officers, engineers, and other low-level officials, who has lost both shame and conscience, and who is ready to sell everything and everyone not merely for one-tenth of a *tuman* but for the smallest fraction of a tenth.

"You made a mistake, my friend," I repeated. "I have a great deal more in the way of sheep than you imagine."

"We aren't asking for any money for your sheep. What are you talking about?"

"May God have mercy!" Svimon shouted. "Just take what you have to. Why do you drag this on forever?"

"Go away!" the official yelled back, offended at being addressed by the shepherd. "Who do you think you're talking to?"

"You're the one who should be quiet," another shepherd yelled at him. "If you don't shut up, I'll push you off your saddle."

The rider trembled in rage, spit, and then suddenly turned his horse around and headed back to Dzaug. Svimon came up to me and said, "Aren't you pleased? We showed him how to treat us!"

"He probably remembered what happened here last year," the other shepherd chimed in.

"What do you mean?"

"Last year our translator also noticed the six days they took from us and they got into a brawl over it."

"Why didn't you complain to the authorities?" I asked.

"Complain?" the shepherd repeated, smiling. "That's exactly what we did. We complained."

"So what happened?"

"We sat in jail for three days. They fined us for each of those days because we left our sheep behind to graze in their fields."

"Did they fine you for the extra six days on the document?"

"Of course! Why would you expect justice in a matter like this? Who would defend us?"

"But didn't you have any witnesses? Wasn't anyone watching?"

"What witnesses! They handed us a piece of paper and said, 'On this paper is written the date when you arrived.' We can't read and so they put our arrival six days earlier than it actually was. When it came to go to court, all they had to do was present the paper, which testified against us."

"Even if someone had witnessed everything, why would he step forward to declare himself against the tsar?" Svimon asked. "Who wants to get involved in other people's business? They would have arrested him, and what good would that have done?"

"They would have done no such thing!" I exclaimed. "Where is it written that you can arrest a witness?"

"You're lucky!" another shepherd answered. "God and society are on your side. But why should us unlucky ones expect justice? Sometimes, you meet a good person, who might have compassion on your misfortune, but justice is not something the Moxeve is destined to experience. No matter where he goes, he's always to blame."

"If the tongue could speak by itself," Svimon interrupted, "then it would speak the truth. Otherwise, people will speak the truth only to themselves. Who is there to expect justice from?"

While immersed in this conversation we drew near another settlement. I was hoping to change my clothing and continue along the way toward Vladikavkaz, where I would seek out the authorities. I was certain that as soon as they had heard about the horrors I had witnessed along the way, they would take immediate and drastic action. Just imagine my shock when I realized that I was a lone voice crying in the wilderness.

The story of how a general's son had taken a walking stick into his hands and set out to tend a flock of sheep had reached the aristocratic salons of Vladikavkaz long before my arrival there.

Three days later, we left Vladikavkaz behind. Our first encounter with the Cossacks, at the Sunzha settlement, ended in a fight. The Cossacks tried to fine us for using public roads, although by law we had the right to occupy thirty *sazhens* of width on both sides of the road. The law granted us this right, but as for what a law means in practice, when the power to administrate it is granted to those who have no conscience—that's another story. Such administrators always act as they please. The shepherd is subject to their irrational behavior, because he is a mere passerby; he has no one to turn to with his complaint and no means of seeking justice.

That's why the shepherds were forced to behave illegally, just like those who lorded over them. They had to defend their rights with force; otherwise they would be forced to pay a fine far beyond their means. We encountered more than a few such obstacles on every journey to greener pastures. We therefore chose paths that we would legally be allowed to pass without paying any kind of fee.

VII

Thus our journey brought us to the foothills of Braguni itself. We passed a countless number of Cossack settlements. At every single one of these settlements, someone was stationed there to torment us with demands for bribes. The shepherds combined their forces during every attack, and this gave us strength. Whenever it was necessary we cleared the ways for ourselves, always in keeping with what the law had already allotted to us. After many such battles, I began to understand the meaning of the shepherd's morning prayer, "God, protect us from Russian roads!"

Even the peaceful Cossacks knew nothing of hospitality; when we crossed through their villages they kept their doors locked tight.[4] What a difference these Cossack villages presented from the Chechen villages, where

---

[4] This paragraph and the following paragraphs until "It took five weeks" was excised from the Soviet-era Russian translation of Yelena Gogoberidze, *Aleksandr Kazbegi: Izbrannoe* (Moscow: Khudozhestvennoi literaturyi, 1949). The omission begins on p. 46.

even those who had nothing to offer, simple folk, and children, were treated like kings when they arrived as guests. Whether or not the Chechens knew you, they would meet you at the entrance to their village and escort you all the way to its end, just as if they had known you for decades. With smiles and politeness they would ask after your family. After they greeted you, they would ask for *"xabar* from Gurjeti."[5] This was a phrase they used to explain the news they were looking for. Chechen villagers treated Georgian visitors with deep affection and lived in complete peace with them.

You can't imagine the vileness of the soldiers standing guard over the Chechen villages. They passed all day and all night in the taverns, tormenting the locals, selling their wives' clothing while satiating their endless appetites on unattached women.

It is instructive to compare Cossack stinginess with the generosity of the Chechens, whose faces were luminous with joy when they saw a guest approaching. There were no drunkards among them. By contrast, there was never any shortage of Russian women hovering drunk by the tavern doors, muttering while reminiscing over past times, their minds absorbed by vodka.

Often the Russian Cossacks were also drunk. They stood idly by the taverns, waiting to satiate their lustful

---

[5] Here Qazbegi is writing as if from a Chechen point of view. *Xabar* is the Chechen/Arabic term for news and Gurjeti is an abbreviation of Gurjistan, the Persian-Turkic term for Georgia. Since the –eti ending is the Georgian equivalent of –stan, the Georgian text merges these two linguistic strands, Chechen and Georgian.

desires. Their lips hung over their teeth, and they tore out each other's hair, but since a Cossack has no understanding of dignity, such a lifestyle was for them perfectly acceptable and in keeping with the order of things. Many times a Chechen would approach a Cossack standing by the tavern and explain that a woman in his family had been raped by him. The Chechen would ask the Cossack why he was not ashamed of his actions. When the Cossack had no response, the Chechen would beseech the sky. "Allah! Allah!" was their way of expressing amazement that any one could so completely have lost their sense of humanity as the unrepentant Cossack.

It took five weeks for us to reach our destination. We passed the time joyfully. We did not see the sun for more than two days during these entire five weeks due to the intensity of the rain.

Just imagine how happy we were when we reached Grozny. This was the seat of the provincial governor, Eristavi. He was the only one among all the governors who cared about the fate of his subjects. Only Eristavi understood that Chechens were humans, too. All the others instinctively assumed that Chechens were intrinsically evil, and would detain them without taking justice into account. Often they would even send Chechens to Siberia.

I decided to ask Eristavi for a small favor. Judging from previous experience, it was entirely possible that the Cossacks would punish us newcomers who had arrived in the area with, so they would have phrased it, the goal of spreading enlightenment. So I decided to ask him for written permission to settle temporarily wherever we wished, without fear of retribution.

When we finally reached Grozny, I opened my suitcase. It had been wrapped in a carpet as we had been journeying, and that carpet had been buried beneath a *nabadi*. But these precautions had, it turned out, been in vain. The rain had dampened my clothes. Simply from the moisture you could have seen how treacherous our path had been, not to mention how much we had struggled with the local authorities.

Eristavi agreed to my request. He passed a paper with the signature of the local chief to extend our rights to us and allow us to pass to Braguni, and without extracting any bribes or perform any other unlawful deeds.

In the spot we reserved for our flock, which belonged to the Makhan-Yurt settlement, we found a beautiful field with water and a forest. We had brought food from the Chechen settlements along the way. I had frequently roamed through this region, seeking to acquaint myself with the strange ways and customs of the Chechens, and I had seen quite a bit of the unexpected.

When we arrived at the campsite, we set our dogs to guard the flock. We must have presented quite a spectacle to anyone gazing in our direction. The shepherds had an endless store of patience and enthusiasm. Just imagine how in a short time they had managed to build an entire village, with doors, gates, and a stable for the sheep. The walls of the buildings consisted of two layers, between which was an open space into which had been stuck clumps of earth. The shepherds worked tirelessly dawn till dusk. Axes resounded in the forest as the woodcutters laughed, drank, and improvised poems for each other. Time passed quickly in the midst of such festivities.

When the building activities were finished, the daily work began. It filled every day we spent in Braguni. Early in the morning the shepherds would chase the sheep to graze in the fields. By night they would bring them back and settle them in the stable for the sheep. Once in a while, a shepherd would go out onto the field to meet the shepherd of another flock. They would greet each other, sit down together, and open their hearts to each other, speaking of everything they had endured and seen in their lifetimes. That's how they passed the hours.

Sometimes, in the darkness of the night, a neighing could be heard as shots resounded. This usually meant that a horse had been stolen from a Chechen village and someone was trying to recover it. There was one more diversion that occupied our days and kept us up at night: legends of famous shepherds and bandits.[6]

Here I cut my story short. About all that I saw, heard, experienced, and came to understand, I narrate in the tales that follow. These stories will acquaint you with the

[6] Qazbegi uses the word *qachaghi* here for "bandits," referring to a pan-Caucasian institution of the robber who steals from upper classes to help those in need. Qachaghi were ostracized by their own societies, and the word does connote criminal behavior, but in certain contexts it is a term of praise. Many famous Georgian heroes have been *qachaghis*. Qazbegi's novel *The Parricide (Mamis mkvleli)* provides an extended account of one such *qachaghi*, also known as *abragi* (Russian: *abreki*). The most famous *qachaghi* are Arsena Mabdelashvili, Zelimkhan (a Chechen), and, some would argue, Amirani.

character, the customs, and the lives of the peoples of the Caucasus. Closer connections with these Chechens will be inevitable in the not-so-distant future.

Fig. 3. Frontispiece to *Sbornik svedenii o kavkazskikh gortsakh* (Compendium of research on the Caucasus mountaineers), vol. 9. The cover depicts the Darial Gorge, a landscape that figures heavily in "Eliso."

Eliso

Near Vladikavkaz, on a low-lying meadow, a group of carts crammed with furniture stood in a circle, guarded by Russian troops. Fires kindled inside the circle, boiling the common meal for the night. Women prepared food, while old men sat on logs, smoking their tobacco pipes silently. Their nostalgic faces created a dreamy picture against the fire's dimming light. Young people stood to the side, awaiting an imminent, unknown disaster.

It was a perfect, warm night, one of those evenings when a person feels blessed to be alive, when pleasure surges through every coil of every vein. Yet a silence hung in the air like a mysterious grief that breaks speech and kills sound before it is born. From time to time, the breathing of those gathered inside the circle was cut short; they stood gasping, immersed in a silence barren of life, like that of the graveyard. The Chechens, vigorous and joyful by nature, were silent and dull today, full of fear like the air before a storm, on the verge of thunder.

Why did these people, so full of life, become so silent? What made their words stick in their craw? What kind of misfortune had struck to make those, who only a few years before would have carelessly greeted the worst of tragedies, now timid and mute?

When the night first fell, faint words could be heard before they dissipated in the air. Soon, however, even those words ceased and were followed by complete silence. The hum of the *chianuri* suddenly broke this peace, recalling to its listeners the kingdom of the dead. The lonely melody was followed by an incessant buzzing sound. My God, what a voice it was! This complaint poured from the heart's depths, burning those who sang and everyone who listened to them. A gentle breeze carried the sound far away, across the meadow, toward every tree, bush, and blade of grass. Everything it touched trembled, as though nature was conscious for the first time of her power.

The droning of one man became a general drone, and the entire meadow was soon covered with plaintive cries and lamentations of the multitudes. Torn from the mouth, this common voice was an inarticulate rendition of the Chechens' pain. Those who heard it suffered and grieved, but were powerless to break free from its spell.

It was the last farewell of a dying child, saying goodbye forever to his beloved mother. It was as though a ruthless, merciless, and unjust power was taking the child away before his time, before he had a chance to caress his mother. It was the sob of an unhappy mother for her firstborn child, followed by the lamentation of a person whose beloved had died.

This groaning, moaning, and lamentation was all the more bitter because it wasn't only a single person's lamentation over his own misfortune, weeping for somebody forever lost. The trials and tribulations of everyone were compressed in this lament; their blood vessels vibrated as one. Here, a single moan contained the tragedy of an entire people.

The Chechens were saying goodbye to the homeland they had spent their lives fighting for. No father had spared his child, no wife her husband, in order to nurture this land, and now after so many struggles, so many sorrows, so many deaths in vain, they were saying goodbye.

"Where are you, God?" they cried, their eyes directed toward the sky. Receiving no answer, their eyes returned to the earth.

In every corner of these places, their friends had spilled their blood. The Chechens remembered the courage of their long-gone friends as they bid their homeland goodbye. With every place they revisited and every step they took, memories of the past grew stronger. Sorrowful pictures scorched their hearts like a branding iron.

Sometimes words have no place in the expression of grief, and yet the wordless lamentations of a conquered people say more than words garnished a thousand different ways. Any person who has never heard the Chechens' lament has never heard the sound of grief.

Everyone looked with grief at the ruins of their village, at the mountain range of Galashka, where once, long ago, these tormented people had battled proudly and where they had also once relished so many minutes full of pleasure.

What was the reason for their deportation, what crime had they committed, that others would make them suffer so, and punish them with such brutality?

They had done nothing wrong. The Chechens were suffering because there were no limits to the greed of Chechnya's new colonial administration. To possess all of the Chechens' lands, this new administration had to have Chechnya without Chechens. To make themselves rich, they needed to send the rightful inhabitants of Chechnya's territory into exile. Deporting the Chechens was the most effective means of achieving this goal.

II.

One young, beautiful girl kept her distance from this general lamentation. She made her way to the bank of the river, where she sat down alone, propped her tender face, full of grace and exhaustion, on her hands, and cast her gaze into the distance. She was absorbed in her own thoughts. Her eyes burned red from the fire that raged inside her. Her heart's fire seemed all the more intense because she suppressed her tears.

The girl stood apart from the common grief. Her heart was filled with another sorrow. Grief is easier to overcome with friends, but this girl separated herself from the crowd in order to meditate over the misery of her situation.

Her name was Eliso. She was the daughter of Anzor Cherbizh, Imam Shamil's famous *naib*. Anzor had once been famed throughout Chechnya for his courage and loyalty, but he had grown old, and was now broken by the years and by his own grief. He had sacrificed his three sons along with his own health and peace of mind to fight for his country's freedom. Now he had to say goodbye to his homeland forever, to leave his home with his only daughter and make a new life for himself in a strange, unknown country.

Anzor stood motionless by their cart, his brows furrowed, his hands resting stoically on his dagger, and listened to the sad, hopeless singing of the *chianuri*. His youth passed before his eyes, already long ago and far away. He recalled the surprise attacks that he led against the enemy in the company of Shamil. He remembered how they used to drive the livestock of their enemies to their own territories, and how they plundered the Russians, bringing joy to their wives when they returned home, heavy with riches.

Several times, he wiped the cold sweat from his forehead, as though to exorcise painful thoughts from his mind. But his efforts were in vain. The bitter feelings aroused by the memories of his past stirred as strong as ever in his heart.

He remembered the days when he traveled like the wind, when all of Chechnya composed poems in his honor, when merely pronouncing his name meant praise. Burdened by heavy thoughts, he bent his head. The image of his lovely wife in the days of her youth passed before his eyes. She had loved Anzor more than anything or anyone else in the world. Her eyes were constantly fixed on his; she had a talent for anticipating his needs before he was aware of them himself. Anzor remembered his children, whom he had expected to look after him in old age and to bury him. The merciless hand of the enemy had killed them all before his eyes, when they were defending their homeland. Anzor sighed bitterly and wiped his hand across his forehead.

"*La illah ila la la la*,"[7] he moaned the ritual prayer of his people.

He turned his head around, as though trying to shake the grief from his eyes and yelled out to a small boy running not far away: "Kora! Have you seen Eliso?"

"Yes, I saw her," the boy said. "She's sitting by the water. I was there washing my face, and saw her there, all alone and looking sad. So sad." The boy couldn't think of anything more to say and escaped from the awkward situation by running away.

"Sad," Anzor repeated. "Of course she's sad. What does she have to be happy about?"

Anzor bent his head and became lost in thought. A few minutes later, he stood up and announced, "She loves him. She loves him, and I want to separate them. I want to spoil their joy!"

Anzor turned toward the river and started off slowly in the direction of his daughter.

Eliso sat by the river, oblivious to everything but her own grief. She was sad not only because she would soon have to leave behind her homeland, but also because

---

[7] Qazbegi's rendition of the Arabic phrase "*La ilaha illa Allāh*" (There is no God but Allah). This phrase frequently prefaces Chechen songs, and it is known in the Islamic tradition as the profession of faith (*shahada*), the recitation of which is one of the five pillars of Islam.

along with her homeland she would be leaving behind her sweetheart, Vazhia.

Eliso loved Vazhia to madness, ever since the days when Vazhia had started herding his sheep in Chechnya. Vazhia was famous throughout the village as a courageous, loyal, and handsome young man. He was well-off by the standards of the village. Any girl would have been happy to be his wife. But Vazhia was a Christian and Eliso was Muslim, and she knew perfectly well that their families would never permit such a marriage.

Not only was the thought of marriage impossible; Eliso didn't dare to even speak with any one about her feelings for Vazhia. She knew that she would never find anyone to sympathize with her suffering among her own people and therefore kept her heart locked tight.

In days past, if a Muslim fell in love with a Christian, mountaineer customs didn't oppose marriage between them, but now the Christian Georgians had taken the side of the Russian *giaours*, fought side by side with them, and even led them against their Chechen brothers. Now the situation was different. With the help of the Christians, the *giaours* had conquered the Chechens' homeland. Thanks to the Christians, the "cowardly *giaours*" had occupied Chechnya, and cut the Chechens off from their homeland. What kind of peace could there be now between a Christian and a Muslim?

So reasoned every Chechen. After their territories had been stolen from them, every tie with their Georgian neighbors had to be severed forever, and the two tribes, which had once had friendly relations, were transformed into enemies with a vendetta against each other.

As Shamil's former *naib*, Anzor was both smart and resourceful. Like the majority of mountaineers, he regarded the tensions between Georgians and Chechens in his own peculiar way. He felt that those Georgians who had conquered the Chechens had been deceived by false promises, and that those mountaineer Georgians who had formerly been the Chechens' friends had been forced to fight against them. Regardless of his sympathy for his mountaineer neighbors, however, Anzor blamed the current subjugation of the Chechens on these Georgians, and tried to stay as far away from them as possible, both in his heart and in his behavior.

Now, as though fate's only intention was to make him suffer, his one and only daughter had fallen in love with a Moxeve, a Christian Georgian. True, Anzor was not completely certain about Eliso's love for Vazhia, but he had his suspicions.

And why did this love have to interfere in their lives precisely at the moment when Anzor and Eliso had to abandon their homeland forever, when, with trembling hands and a pale face, Anzor set his house on fire, to keep it from being plundered by the Russians? Now they didn't even have a house to live in. In those days, in those grieving and tragic days, his daughter, the only comfort and consolation left to him, had her heart captured by a Georgian, who, whether he intended to or not, would distance her from her father.

Anzor knew that as with any Chechen woman, Eliso would not forget her first love quickly, that her heart would not accept another man. A Chechen woman falls in love slowly and with hesitation, but once she is in love, she is in love forever. The feeling consumes her entire being. Anzor was certain of Eliso's constancy, but he still dreamed of the day when her love for Vazhia would fade. He watched Eliso's face melt by the day. Though she became increasingly sad, she did not complain or say even a word about her sorrows.

Up until this day, Anzor had restrained himself for his daughter's sake, and had not given any sign that he noticed her grief, but today, when he was seeing the mountain peaks of his homeland for the last time, when they were handed over to the heartless and rude soldiers like captured criminals, the heart demanded compassion. Anzor could no longer bear his grief alone. He headed toward his daughter with the intention of asking her to open up her heart to him.

Eliso was so driven to distraction by thinking of her beloved that she didn't notice her father's arrival.

"Eliso!" Anzor said and placed his hand on her shoulders.

Eliso shivered and tried to stand.

"Sit down! Sit down!" Anzor said as he sat down beside his daughter.

For a long while, they sat together silently. Eliso stared at the rolling fields with overcast eyes. At the end of the horizon, tree-covered mountain peaks blended into the distance. Anzor watched Eliso observing this landscape, hoping to decipher every motion of her soul.

Finally, Anzor took out a small satchel made of rags, rubbed a lump of tobacco in the palm of his hand, packed it into his pipe, and struck two pieces of flint against each other. Either the flint was damp or the rocks fit together badly, for the fire refused to kindle. Anzor took the rock out again and rubbed the edges together. When at last the fire caught hold, he took the flint and started to make sparks by rubbing the edges together. Anzor raised his pipe and it caught fire. He smoked for a long time and with such intensity that it seemed like he wanted to abolish the movements of his heart, to kill his feelings, and to numb himself to the bitter melancholy surrounding him.

After more silence, Anzor said gloomily to Eliso, "You pain your father! Why are you so melancholy?"

"I'm not melancholy," Eliso said and rested her sad eyes on her father.

"I see. I see," Anzor said, nodding his head. His voice hinted at his inexpressible grief. Then he added, "You suffer, you are full of grief, and I sit here powerless to help my child."

"Don't grieve for me, my dear father," Eliso caressed him tenderly.

"Do you really not grieve? Do you really not suffer?" Anzor asked his daughter.

"What is the use of lying?" Eliso sighed. "You're right, father."

"Then why do you hide your grief from me?"

"Why should I burden you with my sorrows? I wish I could take all your grief from you and bear it myself," Eliso said and embraced her father.

"Me?" Anzor laughed bitterly. "My days have passed. I already have one foot in the grave. Much has happened to me already. But you're just beginning life. Who knows what fate awaits you? God is great." Anzor finished his speech with a moan.

"Father!" Eliso broke in, "All I want is for you to be at peace. I don't want anything else in life. Just for you to rest."

The old man met his daughter's eyes, but did not say anything in response. Silence reigned between them until Anzor interrupted it with a question: "Why don't you talk to your friends? Why do you spend all your time alone here?"

"What do you want, father? What can I do there?"

"What can you do there? Do you think your friends don't suffer? Do you think that the fire of hell doesn't burn their hearts as well? It burns as much as it burns in you, but, when you're with your friends, grief turns into joy. Over there they play the *chianuri* and celebrate. They cry too. Go over there and cry with them. When you cry in the company of others, your heart finds itself."

"How lucky they are that they can cry!" Eliso said.

Anzor watched his daughter with compassion, furrowed his brows, and put his hand on his dagger. He said, "Woman's job is to cry. Man's job is to seek revenge."

Anzor's sunken, lifeless eyes suddenly sparkled in such a way as to make a man bend his head, unable to tolerate their intensity. He fixed his eyes on his daughter, whose gentle beauty calmed him and dulled the sparks in his eyes. Only his lips trembled.

"Eliso," Anzor said, and continued in a quivering voice, "Why are you so full of grief? What makes you so sad?"

"I don't know."

"Eliso, tell your father what you're hiding."

"I'm not hiding anything from you, father."

"Eliso, why do you poison me with your grief? Your sadness shortens my life."

"I'm not complaining. What else do you ask of me?"

"My God!" the old man said. "I want you to be at peace!"

"I am at peace, father."

"You are not at peace! And this is your tragedy."

"What should I be doing, father? How else can I act?"

"Tell me everything, Eliso. Open your heart to your father. Don't you know that, for me, the sun and the moon revolve around you? Do you really have no pity left for your father?"

"Father, what are you saying? How can I prove my love to you? Tell me that you need me to sacrifice my life for you and you'll see how much your daughter loves you. Just tell me, Papa."

With these words, Eliso threw herself on her father and embraced him passionately. Anzor's words opened the floodgates to the tears she had suppressed for such a long time.

"I know that you love another. Your silence pains me. You say you love me yet you won't tell me why you suffer. You say you love me but don't allow me to help you. Maybe *I* am the reason for your suffering?"

"To suffer for you is a joy!"

"But what is the reason for your misery? Why are you withering from grief?"

"I don't know, father," Eliso said as she clung to her father even more strongly than before.

Her embraces were followed by a silence that Anzor broke with a question: "Maybe you're in love?"

Eliso was stunned into a quick reaction: "I never said that."

In spite of her words, however, her already trembling hands started shaking even more and her heart began to beat so loudly that Anzor could clearly hear its palpitations. Eliso pressed herself against her father, who had served as her shield for all their common life together. She did not dare utter what was on her heart; she wanted her father to read her thoughts without her having to speak them.

"No, you didn't say that, but I understand anyway," Anzor said, shaking his head. "What can we do? Such is life. The hour has struck! The chick must fly away! Open your heart to your father. Tell me who is taking you from me. I swear by my ancestors' graves that I won't stand in the way of your desires. Who is it? Who do you love?"

Anzor pricked his ears and waited with a beating heart for Eliso's answer. He prayed that he would not hear the Moxevian name of Eliso's beloved.

"Father! Why do you want me to tell you everything? Why do you want to penetrate the depths of my heart? I swear that whoever I love, no matter how much I loved him, I would never chose him over you. I would bury my feelings in my heart. I will never, ever, abandon you."

The happy father embraced his daughter, confident that he was loved, and that his child would close his eyes when he died. He asked nothing more of life. But after this first rush of joy, he stood back from his daughter and said, "Wait, Eliso. Don't rush to make promises you can't keep. Just as the grass yearns for the dew of the morning, so a woman yearns for a husband. Everything has its place and time. Tell me, Daughter, who do you love?"

"Isn't it all the same to you who it is?"

"Vazhia?" Anzor waited for Eliso's answer with a trembling heart. He still had some hope left that Eliso's sweetheart was a Chechen.

Instead of answering, Eliso embraced her father, who was so consumed by his fears that he couldn't finish his sentence.

"It's Vazhia, isn't it? Is that why you didn't tell me before?"

"What do you want? Why are you so persistent with your questions? I already swore that I would never leave you."

"Are you going to spend the rest of your life in despair?" Anzor asked.

"I will try—" Eliso cut herself short, then resumed her sentence, "to forget."

"You cannot forget! You will never forget!" Anzor covered his mouth and choked on his words.

"Vazhia is a Christian and I am a Chechen," Eliso said. "I must forget him."

"You must, if such a thing is possible."

"I told you I will do it, father. Believe me."

"Eliso! Listen to me. I once had a flock of sheep that crossed every field in Chechnya without fear. Then the *giaours* came and snatched it from me. I had sheep, and a home that was open to all. My guests didn't even have to ask—I would slaughter a lamb for anyone who visited me. Then the *giaours* attacked my village and took everything from me. I had a home that was a refuge to everyone in trouble, a shelter to everyone in need. Then the *giaours* came and burned everything to ashes. All of this happened with the help of the Georgians. They led the *giaours* on the path to battle. They showed them the way. They even fought alongside them. All I had left were my three sons, you, and my weapons. I ran into the mountains. From there I made plans to revenge their injustice, but when God decides to abandon a man, there's no point in struggling against his will. With the help of the Georgians, the *giaours* found out where I was hiding and slaughtered all three of my sons one after another, right in front of my eyes. God is great! What a day that was for me! To think that I survived after seeing that! Only one comfort remains to me: my sons died bravely. All three of my sons had bullet wounds in their chests, which means that my children did not show their backs to the enemy."

After he finished this last sentence, the old man had to stop speaking. Anzor let out a deep groan and passed his hand across his forehead. It took him a long while before he was able to continue speaking.

"The *giaours* came and attacked me seven times, and seven times I turned them back. If not for the Christians, if not for the Georgians, the *giaours* would never have been able to capture my village. Out of my entire household, I was the only one who survived the attack. And for what did I survive? So that the fires of hell would burn in my heart? I am old. My strength has abandoned me. Now, when I need rest more than anything else, there is no one to look after me. I'm traveling far away from the grave of my ancestors, I'll die far away from my children's bones, and my bones will never touch their bones again. My life is dark! Brotherly tears will never be shed over my abandoned corpse. Now you, Eliso, are my only comfort. You are the only one who will close my eyes when I die. But, if this Vazhia has really captured your heart, if you cannot say no to him, then tell me. You are my last comfort, but I will give up my claims to your heart."

"No, no, father! I will never leave you. Even if my love was a thousand times stronger than it is now, I would never leave you. Time will pass, and I will forget him. Don't you believe me that I will forget him, father?"

Anzor pressed himself against his daughter's breast and began to embrace and kiss her, as Eliso had done to him earlier. Then he gazed at the sky, and, in a quiet, but ardent voice, said, "Thank you God, that you have not taken away from me the last comfort in my life!"

Anzor barely finished his words, when a young man, about twenty years old, with a gun swung gracefully over his shoulder and a Tushetian hat tilted to one side of his head, approached them.

"*Marsha dooghiil*,"[8] the boy greeted them in Chechen as he walked toward them.

---

[8] Qazbegi's note here reads: "Chechen—'greetings.'" Literally, *Marsha dooghiil* means "come in freedom [*marsho*]." The text returns to Georgian for Anzor's response.

54

Eliso sprang to her feet when she heard his voice. Her face turned crimson from shyness, and her head was bent low. She couldn't say a word.

"Greetings to you," Anzor answered, rising to his feet. "Guests are from God. Let's go to our cart. We'll say grace to God with what he has given us."

"The Chechens are famed for their hospitality, but I'm not hungry," said the boy.

"A traveler must always be ready to eat the bread that is offered him, for he never knows where he will eat the next day!"

"You're right," the boy answered. "But I'm hurrying. I'm looking for the famous Anzor Cherbizh. I turned back here when I saw these carts. If any of you are from Anzor's village, maybe you could tell me how to find him."

"Anzor Cherbizh? I am Anzor Cherbizh. But who are you? I don't think I know you. It's dark, and I can't make out your face."

"Anzor!" shouted the stranger, and approached more closely.

"Vazhia!" the old man shouted in surprise.

"Good God! And Eliso is here, too!" Vazhia asked after a short silence. "What's new? Where are you headed? Maybe to the shrine?"

Vazhia stared at Eliso, awaiting an answer. When no one answered his question, he tried again. "Eliso! Where I come from, girls go to the shrine dancing and rejoicing. Why do you sit here so full of gloom?"

"Where I come from, girls dance in times of joy and lament in times of mourning," Eliso answered in melancholy voice.

Vazhia gasped at these words. He was on his way to Anzor's village to rent a home and knew nothing about the deportation. He was planning to marry Eliso that winter. Vazhia took a second look at the scene around him and decided that the Chechens did not look like they were preparing to go to the shrine.

"Anzor, what's going on?" Vazhia asked. His voice was full of fear.

"We're going to Istanbul," Anzor answered in a dry monotone.

These words were so unexpected and difficult for Vazhia to understand that it was a long time before he could speak again.

"Where are you going?" Vazhia muttered at last. "What did you say?"

"Istanbul."

"Istanbul?" Vazhia repeated in confusion, still unable to gather his thoughts or make sense of what he had heard. "Istanbul? Where is that? Are you joking with me, Anzor? Eliso, what's going on? At least you'll tell me the truth."

"What Anzor says is true. We're going to Istanbul."

"Eliso, what are you telling me? Think carefully! What kind of answer are you giving me?"

"You—?" Anzor began, without finishing his question.

"Yes, me! What's the use of hiding it any longer? I love Eliso. Vazhia's heart melts for Eliso. And now you tell me that you and Eliso are going to Istanbul?"

"You love my daughter but, but—"

"I love Eliso, thank God. I need her like fish need water, like birds need air. Oh, Anzor! My life is nothing without Eliso. Why do you destroy my happiness? Why do you take away my life?"

The old man was trembling all over and couldn't give an answer. Before him stood a twenty-year-old boy and his sixteen-year-old Eliso. They had a right to happiness and now they were demanding their right. How could he, an old man, stand in their way?

"Eliso, what do you say?" Anzor asked. "What do you think of what Vazhia says?"

"Eliso, speak to me!" Vazhia burst out. "Otherwise my heart will explode with grief!"

No matter how intensely Anzor and Vazhia pleaded with Eliso for her to speak, she refused to answer. She stood as immobile as a stone, oblivious to the pleading glances cast in her direction. Anzor and Vazhia waited for Eliso to speak with hearts filled with the same kind of fear, though they longed for the opposite answer.

Eliso remained silent. Two contradictory feelings battled against each other inside her heart. On the one hand, she was conscious of her duty to her father. On the other hand, she could not face the prospect of rejecting her beloved. Just a few seconds earlier, it had seemed clear to Eliso that her sense of duty had to win over her love for Vazhia, but when she saw her beloved, an invisible power surged through her body, and when she heard Vazhia's voice, she became the woman that nature had created her to become. Though love had not yet completely captivated her heart, she found it harder than she expected to reject it for the sake of duty.

"Eliso!" Anzor said. "Repeat what you told me just now, about how you would never leave me. Or are you afraid to say that now, in front of him?"

"Father!" Eliso whispered, and become quiet again.

"What did I tell you?" Anzor said. "Why do I bother to even ask? It's as clear as daylight! I should never have believed that you could forget him."

Anzor's knees folded beneath him and he fell to the ground, where he sat sorrowfully for some time while the others stood wordlessly. When Eliso and Vazhia saw Anzor's suffering, their love gave way to compassion for the old father about to lose his daughter.

Anzor finally lifted his head and looked around in despair. His trembling fingers sought an object to take hold of. Anzor covered his eyes with his hands and said:

"Everything is over for me. I'm completely alone. Will I pass the rest of my life in loneliness? No one to pity me! No one to take care of me! Not even my native earth beneath my feet! Everything has been taken from me, everything snatched away."

Anzor turned to Vazhia and continued: "Vazhia! I beg you! Do you understand? Anzor Cherbizh is begging you! Anzor Cherbizh, who never in his life asked any man for a favor. You're a man, Vazhia, a brave man. You'll understand the plea of an old man's heart. Don't take my only comfort in the world away from me in the final days of my life! Why do you complain? You're a lucky boy! You have your people, a place to live, native earth under your feet. You have brothers, you lucky boy. You have a family! You're still young! Many happy moments await you. You'll find many young girls who will dream of becoming your wife. Look at me! I'm just an old man, with one foot already in the grave. I have no one and nothing else in the world besides this girl. If you take her away from me, what will I have left?"

Anzor stopped speaking; his breathing had become sporadic. Only by moving his hands did he indicate the chaos inside his soul.

Eliso's refusal was more than Vazhia could bear. Though he was a good-natured boy and wanted the best for everyone, he could not imagine existence without his beloved and he was willing to fight to have her.

The sight of her father's helplessness cast Eliso into a state of confusion. She pitied her father. Not giving Vazhia a chance to answer, she said in trepidation: "Vazhia! By God, who watches over us and by Mother Earth below, Eliso never loved, loves, or will ever love another man in the way she loves her Vazhia! No man other than Vazhia will have the right to call Eliso his wife." She stopped here, because she was losing her voice.

Anzor moaned bitterly. Vazhia stepped forward joyfully, ready to claim his prize.

"But," Eliso continued, "Eliso will never abandon her father!"

The old man grasped his daughter with trembling hands, trying to draw her face to his parched lips. Vazhia stood up, thunderstruck. He was stupefied and could not understand what was going on around him. His eyes sparkled as though ringed by halos of fire. He felt as if an iron vice was fastened tight around his skull, cutting short the circulation of blood and rendering thought impossible, as though he were on the brink of insanity. He shook his head several times, struck his fist against his heart, cried out in frustration, and ripped the buttons off his shirt.

Leaning on his daughter for support, Anzor stood up, then turned away, trembling all the while. Then, he addressed Vazhia: "Go away peacefully, Vazhia! May God send you good luck and happiness!" Then he turned away, because he couldn't manage to say anything more.

The Moxeve took several steps forward, stretched out his hands and yelled, "Hold on a second, Anzor!"

Anzor stopped.

"You say that you love Eliso, that you want the best for her. What makes you think that I don't love her, that I wouldn't give anything for her happiness? I swear by God that I love her more than you! I will suffer more without her than you will! What is my life without her?"

"Eliso, go with your lover if you want," said her father. "The choice is yours."

"Father," Eliso said. "I already told you that I will never leave you. Why do you torture me like this?"

"Vazhia, did you hear what my daughter said? She has chosen to stay with her father."

"And didn't you hear that Eliso loves me?" Vazhia said. "Didn't you hear her say that she's staying with you, even though she loves me? She will never marry another man or know happiness because of you. Why do you poison her life? Why should you be the only one to rejoice? If this is what you want, you love her less than I do. I would never be able to make her suffer for my pleasure's sake. Thank God, I could never hurt her as much as you."

"You cursed boy!" the old man said, grinding his teeth. "A snake is many-colored on the outside, but a human is even worse inside. You want to make me give you my daughter, you evil boy."

"Father!" Eliso screamed. "Stop it! Why are you cursing him? I told you I would never leave you! What more do you want?"

"So you don't love me anymore, Eliso?" Vazhia grew pale.

"As God is my witness, I love you from the bottom of my heart. But I will never leave my father."

"Without you I have nothing to live for!" the Moxeve shouted.

With these words, Vazhia flung his rifle from his shoulders, cocked the trigger, and placed the tip of the gun on his heart. It was a large gun, the size of his body. He placed his hand on the trigger, preparing to fire.

Eliso screamed and fainted. Anzor ran up to Vazhia and wrested the gun from his hand. The gun fired, but, thanks to Anzor, the bullet flew through the air and landed harmlessly on the ground.

"What do you think you're doing?" Anzor yelled at Vazhia.

"Don't try to stop me," Vazhia said. "I'm going to kill myself. Without Eliso, my life has no meaning."

"Don't you try to stain us with your sins, you miserable boy!" Anzor yelled back. "We don't need your blood on our hands!" At that moment, they noticed Eliso, fallen to the ground. Both Anzor and Vazhia raced to Eliso's body and tried to bring her back to consciousness. They forgot about their earlier troubles. Finally, after a great deal of time had passed, Eliso began to breathe again. Only after they heard her breath did the color return to Anzor's and Vazhia's faces.

"She's alive!" The old man said at last.

"Thank you, Lord!" Vazhia said.

Anzor and Vazhia no longer felt like rivals. They forgot all their grievances against each other; for in that instant, Eliso mattered more to them than anything else in the world.

Eliso quietly wiped her forehead with her hand, sighed, and said weakly: "Where am I? What happened?"

"Don't be afraid, my daughter," Anzor said. "Don't be afraid. You're here with me."

"Oh, Father, what happened? I can't remember anything."

"Nothing happened," Anzor said. "The gun fired and you got scared. That's all."

"The gun?" Eliso rose to stand up, and suddenly everything that had happened in the past few minutes passed before her eyes. Eliso turned her eyes sharply on her father and screamed at him: "What happened? You killed him, didn't you?" Then she turned away and said, "Oh my God, Vazhia is dead!"

She tore her hair in grief. Vazhia ran up to her, gathered her in his arms, and pressed her body against his heart.

"Don't be afraid, my beloved. I'm here by your side and alive. I'm doing just fine."

"My God, he's alive!" Eliso embraced Vazhia and kissed him. "Are you wounded? Are you sure you're alright? Vazhia, how could you think of killing yourself? Don't you pity me at least a little bit?"

"You're everything in the world to me!" Vazhia said.

As they stared into each other's eyes, Eliso and Vazhia forgot whose eyes were watching them; they were consumed entirely by the feeling of love.

The wretched father stood nearby, afraid to speak. He saw now that there was no path other than marriage for Vazhia and Eliso, and that he could have lost his only child instead of gaining a new one. He no longer had the strength or will to stand in the way of their happiness.

Anzor blessed his daughter and new son. Together they swore that on the next day all of Vladikavkaz would hear that Anzor and his daughter no longer planned to go to Istanbul. They would remain in their homeland and live in Vazhia's house. Eliso and Vazhia would get married and Anzor would spend the rest of his life together with them.

After they had reached this decision, they returned home together. From here, they listened again to the heart-killing hum of the *chianuri*, accompanied by the same inhuman drone, the same bitter lament. Until recently, the sun had heated the earth, but night had arrived. Now the waning crescent moon shed its light on hundreds of sick people, lying limp and helpless on the field. Many of them were dying without medical help. One mother, her child on the verge of death, stood as if turned to stone, her eyes flickering madly from right to left, seeking someone from somewhere to come and save her child, who was dying before her eyes.

In another place, a woman writhed on the ground in labor, swaying from side to side, grinding her teeth and calling on God to be a witness to her suffering. Nearby, a father moaned goodbye forever to his children, who were also dying or maybe already dead. With a broken heart, he thought of how he would be buried alone, far away from his family. In every place, there was grief and wordless pleading. The *chianuri* set the tune to a baseline of suffering, accompanied by groans, complaints, and an inhuman drone.

Fig. 4. *Chianuri.*

III.

The brutal, wordless cacophony blended with the Chechens' lamentations. Both sounds ushered in the night and persisted until the dawn rose on their misery. Vazhia had been accustomed to misery and self-restraint all his life. Now he waited impatiently for the sun to rise, so as to rid himself of the horrifying picture before him.

Indeed, who could remain indifferent to such suffering, who could fail to be touched by this grief, aside from those soldiers whom someone had placed in charge of the deportation and whose job it was to insure that the rules were obeyed, peace was maintained, and the operations were carried out successfully? Only they stood cheerful amid the general grieving; only they laughed and made fun of the Chechens' wordless grief. The soldiers were accustomed to life far away from their homeland, their people and their hearth. They felt nothing in the presence of other people's grief. Used to a life of aimless wandering, they couldn't understand what this honest and patriotic people were complaining about. All their life, they had moved from one place to another at the behest of those who did not even know their names. Enslaved to what they didn't understand, the soldiers had no wishes or dreams of their own; they lived according to the orders of others and thought that the entire world should live like they did. They didn't understand that not all people are slaves.

It did not take long for the sun to illuminate the meadow. In the forest close by, the chirping and singing of birds paid homage to nature's power. The dew had turned to frost during the night and was now glistening under morning rays. The meadow was full of the scent of newly blossomed flowers. The sun's rays intermingled and bathed the dew in a thousand different shades.

The more stunning the beauty of the landscape, the more flawless it was to the unsuspecting observer, and the more it cheered the hearts of those who didn't know any better, that much more bitter did it seem to those facing deportation, that much more did they feel their own misery. Those Chechens who were able to fall asleep the night before were now awoken by the rays of the sun. Everyone reluctantly prepared their carts and livestock, which small boys had taken to pasture, and pointed them in the direction of Istanbul.

The Chechens were trapped in a kind of paralysis. They had forgotten their first step, what they had come there for and what they were supposed to do. A thousand times, with spinning heads, they searched for sticks to herd their sheep, or for other tools for their carts, not seeing that they were holding these very tools in their hands. If they set out to fulfill some business, an invisible power would stop them and again sadness would descend and they would remain silent until good-natured neighbors or a soldier's order brought them back from their oblivion.

"Anzor, I'm going to Vladikavkaz," Vazhia said at the break of dawn. "While you're on your way to meet me, I'll ask the governor for permission for you to stay behind. So be ready to leave."

"All right," Anzor said flatly.

"It would be nice to see Eliso before I go," Vazhia added with hesitation.

"Eliso has just fallen asleep in the cart. The poor girl! Don't wake her."

Vazhia sighed and set off for Vladikavkaz. His first stop upon arriving in the city was the governor's house. After an interminably long wait for the great master, the governor finally came outside to speak to him. He walked up to Vazhia, who took off his hat respectfully, and said:

"Who might you be?"

"I am a Moxeve, your honor," Vazhia said.

"What did he say?" the governor asked in Russian, a translator standing ready by his side. "What does he want? He's probably been caught thieving, the bastard. My God! When will I be free of these wretched people forever?"

Vazhia understood a little Russian, and he answered proudly, "I'm not one of them. No one can accuse me of being a thief because I haven't done anything wrong! I came to Vladikavkaz on business, and I want to speak to you about it."

"What kind of business? Tell me quickly! I don't have time for you."

"I know an old Chechen who shouldn't be deported. I came here to ask you to let him go."

"Get out!" the governor shouted, when Vazhia's request was translated back to him.

"Why are you angry?" Vazhia asked. "The old man has no one in the world other than his daughter, whom I love."

"If I had my way, I'd deport every last one of you. Do you hear me? I'd get rid of all of you forever. And you're asking me to set free someone who's already on the list? Are you crazy? Get out! I don't ever want to see your face again."

"But your honor—!" Vazhia tried one last time but he was cut short.

"I told you to get out! I have no time for you."

"Then who do you have time for?" Vazhia asked angrily. "I came here on business, to speak to you, and you don't have time to speak to me?"

"Hey, Cossacks," the governor yelled, pointing to Vazhia. "Attack him with your whips!"

Vazhia turned pale and jumped back. "Don't stain me with your crimes!" he shouted at the Cossacks as he placed his hand on his gun.

The Cossacks surged toward Vazhia to attack him, then, suddenly, they stopped short and jumped back. The governor rushed back inside, his heart on fire and full of fear. At first, the Cossacks were scared to lay hands on Vazhia, but then they remembered who they were and were ashamed to think that one man had been able to strike such fear into their hearts.

"Catch him! Catch him!" They shouted and rushed for Vazhia, who cocked the trigger of his gun and stood ready to fire.

"Go away!" Vazhia yelled. "You have no reason to attack me."

"Put down your weapon!" The Cossacks yelled back. "Surrender or you'll be sorry!"

"Cry as much as you want," Vazhia said. "While Vazhia is alive he'll never put down his gun."

"Guns! Guns!" several of the Cossacks shouted while the others ran to get them. This entire scene took place on the balcony. Vazhia saw that the Cossacks were also standing at the bottom of the staircase. He realized then that he wouldn't escape alive. He did not want to sell his life cheap, and decided to die nobly.

"You dogs!" Vazhia yelled. "Twenty against one and you think you're brave? If you're so strong, why don't you come against me one by one? Then we'll see whose mother will cry."

Vazhia had no wish to shed blood for its own sake, but the Cossacks left him with no other choice. He prepared to die. At the very moment when he had abandoned all hopes of being saved, Vazhia glanced behind him and noticed a window left open, which looked onto the road below. Without giving himself time to think, he placed his hands on the frame and jumped out the window.

A Cossack below was out walking the governor's horses, in preparation for another tour of the Chechens' camp. Vazhia approached the Cossack, snatched him up like a small child, and dropped him to the ground. Then he mounted the best horse and spurred it toward the forest.

The stupefied Cossacks rushed toward the window in pursuit. No one was brave enough to jump onto the grass below. They managed to shoot two or three times into the air before Vazhia's figure vanished from their horizon. A second group of Cossacks hurried down the stairs, mounted their horses and set off at a gallop after Vazhia, who had crossed the field and was making his way for the forest. At first, the Cossacks chased him as a group, firing their guns and galloping at the same time.

Soon, however, several horses raced ahead of the others. A few minutes later, just two horses were at the front, speeding out of the field of vision of the other Cossacks. Soon, only one horse and his rider remained at the front, galloping at the speed of lightning in pursuit of Vazhia. Those who straggled behind stopped firing their guns; they were afraid that their bullets might hit the Cossack who had vanished into the distance.

Meanwhile, Vazhia raced forward on his horse. He shouted and waved his hat, but the horse was well-fed and too used to a life of luxury. She began breathing heavily and then suddenly slowed down. The horse of the Cossack chasing him galloped forward without slowing down; her sleek, lean thighs moved freely, each leg gliding past the other. The Cossack didn't have a gun with him, but his wild and inflamed eyes revealed his fury. When I capture Vazhia, they seemed to say, I'll rip him to pieces.

At last, the Cossack's horse came even with Vazhia's. Vazhia realized that he would not make it to the forest in time. The Cossack's companions reached the edge of the field and yelled battle cries in the direction of their leader. Their tones and movements were cautious; they carefully kept a safe distance between themselves and the battle they screamed for.

Vazhia glanced behind him and saw the Cossack take out his sword and lunge toward him. Vazhia lifted his gun and took aim. The Cossack lay flat on his horse and the bullet flew past him, only scraping his hat. Then he sat back up on his horse and shouted in triumph. Vazhia had no time to load his gun again, so, regarding it as a useless weapon, he flung it back over his shoulder and took out his sword. One second more and the Cossack's sword would have reached him, but Vazhia turned his horse to the side just in time, and the Cossack's sword slashed through empty air.

The fight took place so fast that neither Vazhia nor the Cossack had time to think. The Cossack's horse rushed forward, and Vazhia sat up on his mount. The Cossack's horse stood on her hind legs, as though forced to attention by her master. The Cossack swayed, bent over backward, and hung onto his horse. Then the stirrups slipped from his feet and he fell to the ground. Only then was it clear that Vazhia's sword had penetrated the Cossack's skull.

The Cossack's horse, happy to be freed from her master, curled her lips and started chewing on the grass at her feet. Vazhia turned his back on his own horse and took the reins of the Cossack's horse in his hands. He rode the new horse into the forest and hid there, under cover from the waves of bullets the Cossacks were firing in his direction. Only after Vazhia had managed to conceal himself safely inside the forest, did the remaining Cossacks reach the end of the field. They looked long and hard for him but all their searches were in vain; Vazhia was nowhere to be found.

When the governor found out what had happened, he shouted to his Cossacks, "Didn't I say that they were cursed by God? I don't care what it takes and how hard we have to try, we must get rid of them all as soon as possible!"

"Yes, sir! Yes, sir!" the Cossacks repeated, nodding their heads vigorously to signify their submission to the governor's will.

Thus they marked their support for the will of their master, thus they created the illusion of their agreement. These were the Cossacks who rejoiced at the deportation of the Chechens, and who were prepared to do the same to the Georgians should the opportunity arise.

IV.

The Chechens continued on their way toward Vladikavkaz. The carts' wheels lazily screeched against the earth, drilling holes into the Chechens' hearts. Barefoot children followed behind the carts, their feet split into pieces by the heat and the sharp, brittle rocks mixed in the sand. The dust had settled inside the gashes in their feet, marking uneven blue lines on their flesh. After every step, they lifted their feet from the ground, so as to keep their soles from touching the rocks. The children's limping walk merely hinted at their pain. Even when they managed to suppress their cries, they still moaned and grimaced bitterly.

Thus they made their way toward Vladikavkaz, where they were greeted with commiserating frowns and compassionate stares. Everyone knew they were being tortured, but what could they do? What could lighten their suffering?

Eliso suffered as she waited for Vazhia. The Moxeve was nowhere to be seen. It was as if Vazhia had forgotten his sweetheart, the very same girl for whom yesterday he had tried to kill himself.

Nor did Anzor know anything of Vazhia's adventures. He was surprised when Vazhia failed to meet them when they reached Vladikavkaz to take them to the governor as they had agreed beforehand. Eliso and Anzor descended the spirally road like lambs headed for the slaughterhouse. They avoided each other's eyes, afraid to remind each other of their grief by an unexpected question or an involuntary gesture. What was the point of speech, when everything was so clear anyway? Vazhia had promised to meet them at the entrance to Vladikavkaz. They had already passed the entrance to Vladikavkaz and now they had reached its end, but the Moxeve was nowhere to be seen.

The Chechens reached the place where they were to stay for the night and stopped their carts. The soldiers encircled them. Several Cossacks appointed themselves as guards.

The sun had not yet set by the time the governor arrived at the camp, accompanied by a train of Cossacks and subordinate officers. When he reached the Chechens, he called them together and said: "All of you expressed your wish to immigrate to Turkey and we granted you your wish. Now a rumor has reached me that some of you wish to stay behind. I therefore announce to you that those who have been written in the list of those to be deported will remain on that list forever. None of you have any hope of escaping. I have multiplied the soldiers and Cossacks assigned to you. Anyone who attempts to escape will be killed mercilessly. These are the orders my Cossacks have received."

With these words, the governor kicked his horse's thighs and sped away. His entourage imitated their leader and set off at a brisk trot toward Vladikavkaz.

After the governor was gone, the Chechens dispersed with quiet moans. What could they say? Who would have understood their grief? After the shock of the news had died away, they set about pitching their tents for the night.

It was about nine o'clock when they finished their preparations for the evening. The assemblage of deportees presented a scene similar to that of the night before. Fires sparkled here and there, and men and women raced back and forth like shadows. The only difference was that now the Chechens were even sadder and more distraught by grief. The *chianuri*'s voice could be heard no longer. The only sounds which resonated without interruption were the inhuman drone, the moaning, the pleading, and the lamentation of the soul, which could not express itself in language.

For the last time in their lives, the Chechens stared at their mountains and the valleys which covered their horizon as far as their eyes could see. They sent a silent, sad, farewell in the direction of their homeland. As for the rest of their grief, it was contained in their moaning and the incessant buzzing noise that arose from their surroundings.

Suddenly, a dust cloud swirled overhead. It felt as though the source of the wind was beneath their feet. The mist rose like smoke and immediately dispersed. In a place not far away, the mist rose again and dispersed just as suddenly. In several more spots, the mist rose from the earth and faded into the air.

The wailing of the wind merged with the incessant buzzing. The cries of the mother who would never see her firstborn children again remained as inconsolable as before. The wind calmed down for a moment, but its peace was a deception. Within the next second, the sky was blanched the color of bullets, and prepared for an explosion. It was as though nature was finally moved to tears by the suffering of its wretched creation and the sky wanted to issue a final farewell to its children before their departure for another country, shielded by an alien sky.

The wind stopped wailing. The heat rose. A silent pall cast itself over everything and the air grew dense. The Chechens breathed more slowly, and began to cough. One drop fell, followed by a second one. A hesitant rumble of thunder broke the silence, followed by a thin, pale streak of lightning. The rain fell incessantly. One second later, the green meadow was covered in water, on top of which grass floated, swaying in suppressed agitation. The water collected in pools in the uneven patches of the ground because the satiated earth could no longer absorb water. From time to time, the cold wind wailed across the landscape, turning everything to ice. Lightning and thunder joined the wailing of the wind and the incessant buzzing sound.

The children cried, tormented both by fear and the cold weather. A woman in labor moaned and cursed those who had placed them there. Mixed into her curses were the sighs of an exhausted soul. Men with furrowed brows and their hands on their daggers stood quietly and watched their lives pass before their eyes. They were still waiting for justice to appear, but from whom?

In one corner of the settlement, a sick old woman shivered from the bitter cold. Her clothing was ripped open in places to reveal red flesh. She was lying in a muddy pool and struggling against death. Up until the last moment of her life, her soul could find no relief.

The rain continued to fall. Anzor noticed the ragged old woman and covered her with his coat. A group of children gathered next to her and, shivering, lay down beside her like guardian angels and prayed for her soul. Several seconds later, the old lady made an effort to sit up, and, greedy for life, gulped down the air until it choked her and she died.

Is it possible that God didn't feel anything, that he didn't look down from his high place in the skies and pity his creation?

Once the rain had extinguished all the fires, the dark night turned pitch black. A deathly silence reigned, violated only by the thunder which raged at rare intervals and by the rhythms of the Chechens' lamentations and their pleas for help addressed to a God who didn't answer.

At about ten o'clock, a mysterious figure could be discerned making his way through the grass toward the Chechens' settlement. He moved forward on all four limbs in almost complete silence, crawling like an insect through the field. Every so often, he would stop, peep his head over the grass, and survey the scene. As soon as he made sure that his movements were not noticed by anyone, he would lie back down in the grass and resume crawling forward. When he approached the place where the guards surrounded the camp, he quietly stood up. His eyes were accustomed to the night. He observed that a soldier was approaching close to him; it would be difficult to pass by without being noticed.

Thanks to the bad weather, the soldier was standing hunched over and with his eyes shut tight, waiting impatiently for his shift to end. All of a sudden, he opened his eyes and stood back. He seemed to have noticed the figure crawling in his direction and opened his mouth to shout, but exactly at that moment, Vazhia pressed his dagger against the soldier's throat, cutting short his scream. The soldier fell down and began fidgeting like an epileptic.

Vazhia quietly cleaned his dagger in the damp grass and resumed crawling in the direction of the Chechens. When he approached the carts, he stood up and entered the settlement fearlessly. He located Anzor's cart by asking the Chechens on the outer ring of the settlement. Eliso had taken refuge from the rain inside the cart. Only Anzor was standing outside, bare-headed. His hair was a tangled mess. Oblivious to the bad weather, he was completely absorbed by grief. Now, when Vazhia and his daughter were so intensely in love that separating them would mean their death, he felt that he might have to sacrifice his life if that was the only way for them to stay together.

"Hey! You over there!" Anzor said suddenly, when he saw a mysterious figure approaching him, still shrouded in fog. "Who are you?"

"Anzor? Is it you?"

"Vazhia!" The old man yelled with joy and ran up to greet him.

"We need to hurry if we're going to escape." Vazhia said.

Life had taught Anzor that there was no point in wasting time with useless formalities in such situations.

He skipped the greetings which politeness demanded. "What about the soldiers?" Anzor asked. "Where will we escape to?"

"I have horses ready for us a short distance away," Vazhia said. "We'll make it. But hurry!"

Had Anzor been alone, he would not have thought twice about following Vazhia, but his daughter, his last consolation and the meaning of his life, was with him. Anzor would chose death rather than endanger his daughter's life.

"What about my daughter? God forbid—"

"I'm ready," Eliso broke out, as she emerged from the cart. "I heard everything and I am ready. Let's go."

"Eliso!" Vazhia cried out, and pressed his sweetheart to his chest.

Anzor watched the picture with teary eyes. His was afraid of interrupting their joy with a reminder to hurry, so he waited to let them savor the moment.

"Let God unite what man is powerless to separate!" The old man finally said. He knew well the price of every second of delay, and added, "Hurry! Now that we've decided to go, we need to leave."

These words brought the lovers back from their oblivion. They remembered the unfortunate reality, and knew they had to act fast.

"You're right," Vazhia said. "There's no point in de-laying." He wiped the dirt from his clothes, took off his hat, and added, "Gods of Xevsuretia, and holy angels of the cross, protect and watch over us!"

They set out along the same path that Vazhia had used to reach them with Vazhia in the lead. When they passed all of the carts, Vazhia said to Anzor, "From here on, we have to crawl on our stomachs."

The men lay down on their stomachs. Eliso lay down between them, and all three began crawling forward. Thus they passed the soldiers guarding the camp unnoticed. They soon saw three horses waiting for them on the edge of the Tergi River. Anzor, Vazhia, and Eliso mounted the horses and sped off toward the mountains.

V.

Their horses galloped as fast as they could manage, leaving Lars and the Darial Gorge behind as quickly as possible. They crossed the most hazardous spots, where the rocks were split as if on purpose to deprive the passerby of all means of freely walking across. In those days, crossing the mountain was more difficult than in times past, as the whole mountain in all its width and breadth was covered with Russian soldiers, who had been given free reign to perpetrate any kind of injustice they wished. No one witnessed the actions of these soldiers. No one was stationed in the mountains to monitor their behavior, and thus there was no punishment for their crimes.

It was about midnight when Vazhia and his companions approached the most dangerous spot in Lars. Vazhia, who had earlier been leading the way, suddenly pulled his horse to a stop and jumped off. Anzor and Eliso followed his example and stopped their horses.

"What's going on?" asked the old man.

"Jump off your horses!" ordered Vazhia, as he helped Eliso descend from her horse.

Anzor gave the horses' reins to Vazhia and didn't bother to repeat his question. Vazhia's imperative manner indicated the danger of their situation. There was no time to lose.

Vazhia removed his leather cloak from his saddle, took out a knife, and began cutting the cloak into small pieces. Then he took a thin rope out of his sack and fastened patches of leather to the horses' hooves. Anzor had spent his entire life in the plains and had no experience with steep landscapes. He didn't understand Vazhia's cautionary tactics and watched his actions with surprise.

"What on earth are you doing?" Anzor finally burst out, unable to restrain his curiosity any longer.

"Guards are posted everywhere and we're riding over limestone!" Vazhia answered.

From these words, Anzor deduced that Vazhia was tying the horses' feet with the soft leather in order to muffle the sounds of their steps. As an old warrior and leader of troops, Anzor was pleased by this idea.

"You're a smart young man!" Anzor said. "It's a pity that Shamil was captured. You could have made a great name for yourself by fighting alongside him!"

"Sit down!" Vazhia ordered. Within a few seconds they were back on the road.

Previously, the clip-clop of the horses' hooves on the limestone had been loud enough to wake the dead. Now their movements were nearly inaudible.

As he proceeded further down the road, Vazhia grew more confident that he had deceived the guards. The weather promised to be as bad as ever, and the mist lay low on the ground. It was so dark that a man strolling through these regions would not have been able to make out the fingers in front of his eyes.

Vazhia, who had until this point raced forward, suddenly froze. He pricked his ears forward and stopped moving, in order not to miss a single sound. Several times, he would stop his horse, and thrust his neck and ears forward. Once he was convinced that no danger lurked ahead, he would continue his journey forward.

They approached a bridge that stretched over the Charxi River. The horses brayed and stepped backward. Vazhia cursed his horse and spurred her forward, then tried to maneuver her across the bridge, but she resisted. He stepped forward tentatively, and immediately jumped back. A fire flashed like a thousand tongues and the thunderous roar of several guns was heard.

"I'll be damned! What's that?" Vazhia barely managed to ask his question before he broke out, "You dogs!"

He shouted and reined back his horse. A sudden bolt of lightning illuminated tens of armed Russians. Vazhia unsheathed his sword and lifted it in preparation to strike his enemies, but he soon felt the cold prick of a spear pierce his heart. His body convulsed, he staggered, and fell to the ground.

"You have no God, no justice, no faith," he said as he lay dying. "Eli—, Eliso." And with these words he gave up his soul.

Anzor and his daughter remained at a distance from this scene. They too were scarred by bullets. Before his

81

death, the old man managed to embrace Eliso for a final time. He pressed her hard against his chest. With his arms wrapped around his daughter, he died.

Three days after the deaths of Vazhia, Anzor, and Eliso, the other Chechens reached the place at the foot of the road where the bodies of the dead had been thrown. Their corpses still lay there; no one had thought to bury them. Now the Chechens were even more grieved than before. Again the inhuman drone, again the moaning, again the weeping and lamentation, torn from the depths of their hearts and dissipated into the air. They set out for the Ottoman Empire, but how many of them ever reached their destination?

1882

Eliso

Fig. 5. Darial Gorge, near to the location of Vazhia's death. Painting by Ivan Aivazovsky (1862). This gorge marks the border between Georgia and Russia, and it has come to epitomize the difference between Russo-European civilization and Caucasian mountaineer barbarism for writers as wide ranging and Mikhail Lermontov, Ilya Chavchavadze, Titsian Tabidze, and Boris Pasternak.

Fig. 6. Mount Qazbeg by sunlight, overlooking the region of Xevi below.

Fig. 7. Cminda Sameba (Holy Trinity Church), with two men and a
boy in the foreground. Photograph (c. 1880–1890)
by Italian photographer Vittorio Sella. Reprinted with permission of
the Georgia Central State Audio-Visual Archive.

Xevisberi Gocha

I.

I t was about nine in the evening when several armed
men in sleighs and horses approached the village of
Qanob. The riders were young and attractive. They
rejoiced as they traveled, singing and shooting their guns.
They rushed forward on their sleighs as if they didn't
have a care in the world. Thus they made their way, full
of courage and hope, toward an isolated village in Xevi,
which was so well fortified by the mountains that no
one could seize it by force.

As soon as they reached the village, they were met
with shouts of joy and gunshots by a group of local boys
and men on horseback. The riders raced forward with
dizzying speed, bent backward, and fired their guns in
different directions. Still mounted on their horses, they
bent down to the earth, supported themselves on their
hands, straightened up like arrows, and sped toward
each other. They came so close that they nearly crushed
each other. Then, suddenly, with an uncanny synchro-
nicity they froze. Finally, they opened their mouths and
shouted with joy:

"May your path be peaceful!"

"May your travels be safe!"

After the ritual exchanges of greetings, the two groups merged together and walked to a house standing on the edge of the village. The light of a fire streamed out from the windows of the house and joyous sounds of the *panduri* accompanied the dancing and singing. More guns resounded from the door. The thunder of gunshots united with the excited shouts of children. The riders dismounted from their horses. The children took hold of the horses' reins and walked them back and forth to keep them warm and to dry the sweat streaming down their backs. Otherwise, the icy breeze would have frozen them to death.

The guests gathered by the door. A good-looking youth, on whose face stubble had just began to appear for the first time, stood in the middle of the circle, his *nabadi* thrown across his shoulders. He was followed by another youth, dressed more elegantly than the first, in layers of gold and silver.

Silence fell over the room, a silence so complete that even the buzzing of a fly could be heard. Suddenly, a high-pitched, clear voice began singing from somewhere far away: "Zhvaruli" was the name of the song. Other voices joined in the singing. Polyphony sweetened the air with a harmony that made everyone tremble.

"Zhvaruli" is only sung in the mountains, for only in these regions can such powerful harmonies be born, and even then only during war, religious festivals, and weddings. The occasion this time was a marriage. Gugua Pichitauri, the man dressed in a *nabadi*, was the groom of the wedding. By his side, decked in gold, stood Onise, the son of the esteemed Xevisberi Gocha, Gugua's best man and friend.

II.

The guests entered the house, already crowded with people. The elders came forth to welcome the guests and bless the groom. First, the groom was escorted around the room, and then he, along with his best man and the master of the house, sat together by the hearth burning in the center of the room. The men seated by the fire there drank once again from their bowls of beer. Then they sang poems to each other.

The youths gathered around the young girls dancing in one corner of the room and stared with amazement as they moved their bodies in rhythm with the music. Everyone was in a playful mood. The boys tried to seduce the girls by dancing. A boy dressed entirely in black blinked his eyes mischievously, and again, excited and emboldened by some mysterious force, chased the dancing bodies which were at times quiet and graceful as the ripples in a river, and at other times angry as a rabid dog and full of treachery.

One black-eyed Moxeve girl danced like an intimidated mountain goat. Her face filled with fear, as a man lunged toward her like a hungry eagle in pursuit of his prey. The gentle creature gradually became inert, her dancing partner caught her up in his arms, as she began to tremble like a dove. Within a moment, however, she turned away and slipped from his grasp, leaving him with his desires frustrated and unfulfilled. Then she jumped to her feet and started dancing on the opposite side of the room. Full of resentment, the man stared at his victim, who looked back at him with an enchanting smile. His shimmering, provocative eyes seemed to say, "Capture me and I'll make you feel the sweetness of life!"

For Onise and Gugua, this was the most solemn day of their lives. They sat together motionlessly, and stared quietly at the young men drinking and feasting. However, their hearts accompanied the young boys caught up in merriment. Gugua was consumed by a single wish: to catch a glimpse of his beloved Dzidzia. Onise, meanwhile, searched the room in vain for the girl with lightning in her eyes, rosy lips, the tinge of innocence in her cheeks, and through whose veins the blood of life flowed.

Soon, the dancing slowed down and everyone divided into two groups. An old woman emerged from the crowd and made her way toward Onise. The guests greeted the old woman as she approached Onise and embraced him.

Then the old woman said, "My everything, my all! I entrust my daughter to you. Kill anyone who hurts her! Look after her, like a best man should."

"You can't hide anything from God, Xazua. God willing, I'll do everything you ask," Onise said, and added in a serious tone, "I'll make trouble for anyone who makes trouble for Dzidzia. I don't advise anyone to fool with me."

"Gugua is still small," the old woman began. "The world is wide. A man's tongue can say anything. Guide this young man. Don't let him follow others' words blindly. Don't let the enemy kill him or convert him to foreign customs. I entrust you with my daughter. Treat her well."

"What are you saying, Xazua?" Onise interrupted. "Gugua is indeed still young, but he is a sober and obedient boy. Everyone is honored to have him as a friend. They would sacrifice their lives for his sake, because they know that Gugua would do the same for his friends. Gugua's a brave man, and, thank God, his family has no reason to feel ashamed of him."

"May your words come true!" the old woman said just as the ritual dictated, and added, "Don't get angry, Onise. I'm as old as the sky, and Dzidzia is the anchor of my soul. For me, the sun and the moon revolve around her."

"That's all good and well, Xazua, don't bore your guests," an old man shouted from the crowd, "Now it's time to take him to the bride."

"Yes, indeed, you're right, my dear," Xazua said. "Onise, go ahead!"

Gugua followed this exchange with his eyes filled with envy. He knew that, according to the customs of the mountains, he had to keep his distance from Dzidzia. Many hours still had to pass before he would be able to touch her face.

III.

It had barely grown dark in the pantry where the women waited when a small fire was lit, illuminating the entire room. Among the jugs and wine barrels sat Dzidzia, the bride, with several of her closest friends, trying to amuse her. Their efforts were in vain.

Dzidzia was sixteen years old, on the verge of womanhood. She had only recently blossomed. She was at that age when the body grows restless and passion floods the veins and, like a torrential river, threatens to take over the soul. At that age, a girl's heart yearns for an unknown happiness; life spreads itself before her like Eden, promising undiluted pleasure. At that age, girls believe that they will find love.

Dzidzia was a beautiful girl. She had a good figure and wonderful lips, as small as flower buds, so attractive they seemed to ask to be kissed. A pale hint of red played on her white skin, as soft as silk. Her cheeks were not red like the other village girls; she possessed a different kind of beauty. Her gentle blue eyes were both pure and tempting. They would strike an arrow into the heart of anyone who gazed into them. Her long black eyelashes stood guard over her long, thin, velvet eyebrows.[9] Her thick black hair was rolled into two braids which wrapped like ivy around her neck, as fragile as crystal. In short, everyone who had the pleasure of looking at Dzidzia could not keep from exclaiming: "Blessed be your parents for having borne such a child as you!"

Many young men in the village were attracted to Dzidzia. Several had even tried to kidnap her, but it seemed that she was fated to marry Gugua and to remain his forever. Now that Gugua had named Dzidzia as his own, now that Dzidzia had promised to become his, no one else could declare his love. Everyone knew

[9] The personification of eyelashes seems to have been imported into Georgian from Persian poetry.

that Gugua was not much given to joking and that he would kill anyone who tried to stand in the way of his fulfilling his dreams.

Dzidzia was marrying according to her wishes, and though she liked Gugua very much and though there was not a single night during which she did not stay up late, losing sleep in anticipation of their marriage, though many times she conjured up in her imagination Gugua's lionlike countenance and brave figure, still, today, when it was time for her to say goodbye to her home, her friends, to everything she held dear, when it was time for her to take her first step away from girl-hood and toward womanhood, her heart trembled. She became absorbed by nostalgia for her past. Memories of those days when she had been coddled and caressed by everyone began to consume her. Who knew whether the future held in store for her the same kind of love?

Dzidzia only felt a vague, mysterious sense of agitation. She could not articulate what was going on inside her. This uncertainty stole the color from her face, and it rendered her as pale as an angel.

Her friends were busy trying to cheer her up by joking with her, when suddenly someone announced: "The best man is coming! The best man is coming!"

The guests jumped to their feet. Dzidzia felt as though someone had stabbed her. An unpleasant feeling filled her soul. She covered her face with a veil and stood up.

Xazua entered the room, along with an elderly man, Onise, and several young women, who ran up to

Dzidzia and embraced her. They prepared her to say goodbye to her past life and with tears and kissing bade her farewell.

Finally, the singing stopped, the old man lit a candle, made the sign of the cross, went over to the woman and took her hand, appealed to the gods of Xevi, and turned to Onise: "Onise! I entrust you with this shy, innocent woman. From this day forth, you are to look after her as you would your own brother." With these words, the old man placed Dzidzia's burning hand into Onise's.

As soon as Onise felt Dzidzia's hand on his palm, he shuddered, though he could not have explained to himself what made him tremble.

"From this day forth, it is your duty to look after this poor, defenseless girl. She has no one else in her new village to look after her. You must be her brother."

"May God be my witness," Onise solemnly pronounced, "I will never abandon her."

Onise then stepped closer to Dzidzia and raised the veil over her eyes. Then he intoned: "She is my sister and I am her brother."

He couldn't complete his sentence, and stuttered like a drunken man. Somehow, he recovered his balance and managed to stand straight.

"What's wrong?" The old man came up to help him. "Are you alright?"

"I'm fine," Onise mumbled. "I'm just feeling a bit dizzy."

"Have you been drinking a lot?" the old man asked Onise then turned to the spectators: "Someone bring some water quick!"

"I'm fine. I don't need water." Onise clasped Dzidzia's hand, though it made his blood boil, and made him feel like he was losing his mind.

Onise passed his hand across his forehead, to wipe the sweat away. He gazed into Dzidzia's eyes and said in a loud, firm voice: "May the gods in the heaven above and the earth below be my witness, that I will love Dzidzia like a sister. I'll be a brother to her. I'll love her more than a brother!"

Dzidzia's hand trembled again at these words. Again, she quietly shuddered, cast a shy glance in Onise's direction, and immediately lowered her head. Onise's timid but powerful moaning deprived him of the power of speech and filled his heart with desires for which he had no name.

Onise's blood rushed through him as waves at high tide race toward the shore and back toward the sea. His heart beat at a maddening rate, like a boat without a mast wandering amid the waves. Then the blood struck his head and wrapped it in mist. Everything went dark before his eyes. Onise was angry at himself that he had allowed this feeling to weaken his heart, that he had not been strong. He was powerless to control his newly aroused passion. For Dzidzia's sake, he pretended that everything was fine with him, but the illusion was hard to maintain. His mouth was parched; he felt like his throat was being squeezed in a vice. He realized that it was best to stay as far away as possible from the perilous face which had enslaved his entire being so unexpectedly, and which was now trampling his heart.

IV.

Trays loaded with sweet buns and mutton were stacked on the tables. The guests who remained behind at that late hour continued to rejoice. The young men gossiped among themselves, while the elders passionately debated Georgia's destiny.

Snow from the night before still covered the ground, but the snow kept falling outside. The guests hurried to finish eating quickly and return home. They were afraid that an avalanche along the way might block their path and that the newlyweds would be stuck outside, at the mercy of nature.

The toasting dragged on, while the host and head of the family sat down at the head of the table, lit a candle, and called upon the gods and angels of Xevi to look after and protect the newlyweds. Then he turned to Onise and reminded him of his responsibilities toward Dzidzia and demanded the trunk with the dowry inside. The old man then handed the trunk over to the groom's contingent.

A second later, Onise was escorted to the special room, somewhat like a pantry, where Dzidzia was to be entrusted into his care.

Onise still was unable to understand what was going on around him. He was in a strange situation, completely confused. Yet somehow he managed to perform the rituals that were expected of him. The guests interlocked his hand with Dzidzia's, in keeping with the tradition, and once again the choir began to sing "Zhvaruli." Dzidzia and Onise went inside where Gugua was waiting for them. All of this beautiful singing sounded to Onise like lamentation by the side of a grave, over someone who had recently died. Gugua, standing against the wall, was entirely illuminated by the light of the fire; his eyes sparkled like diamonds. A subdued smile played on his face. He bent his head, lest the pleasure he felt inside became visible.

Onise led Dzidzia to Gugua. When they reached the groom, he turned Dzidzia around to face her husband-to-be, who immediately took her hand. The only thing that seemed strange about this procession was that the bride continued to keep her grip on Onise's hand and would not let go. Gugua resolved the problem by clutching her fingers with such force that Dzidzia's bones cracked and she nearly screamed.

Onise walked in front of the bride and groom, accompanying them to the sleigh, where the bride was supposed to be handed over from the groom to the best man's care. In keeping with tradition, Onise and Dzidzia sat down alone together in the first sleigh.[10] The groom was supposed to arrive on a horse because he was forbidden from contact with the bride until the marriage. His friends placed the trunk with the dowry on the second sleigh. The grooms' guests sang yet again, fired their guns, shouted with joy, and set off from home.

[10] This tradition is no longer followed. Nowadays, the marriage ceremony takes place in the girl's village and the bride and groom are already married before they depart for the groom's village. Because the marriage ceremony has been completed in such cases, and the bride and groom are now man and wife, they can sit together when they travel. [Qazbegi's note.]

V.

Though it was a cold and foggy night, the snow blanched the earth white and lit their path. From time to time the wind whistled shrilly, and stray particles of ice struck the travelers' faces like a whip.

A small boy, wrapped entirely in his *nabadi*, scarf, and hat, spurred the horses forward. Ice covered the road till it became invisible. The horses moved forward with difficulty. They had only just started on their trip, and they still had many miles to cover.

The groom's guests galloped away, leaving Onise and Dzidzia alone, the joyful sounds of celebration resonating in the distance. Their horses sped ahead, racing after each other. Some guests snatched the hats from each other's heads and threw them down to the ground. At the same time, others bent down from their horses and picked up the hats. Thus they passed the time, warm and full of rejoicing.

Onise was comfortably seated inside the sleigh, with his scarf thrown down and his hat tilted to the side. He lifted his hat and pointed his sweating forehead toward the freezing wind.

Whether it was the purity of the air or the passage of time, Onise was finally able to think clearly and analyze his situation objectively. Only now did he taste for the first time in his life the sweetness of the feeling that Dzidzia had evoked in his soul. Only now did he fully understand what had happened to him. Onise felt like the entire world was in his hands; his love had opened up a second life within him. Alongside the pleasure, however, stood the obligation between him and his best friend, Gugua, which weighed heavily on him and impelled him to treat the girl sitting next to him, whom he loved with all his being, with a love more passionate than familial, like a sister, a mere appendage to his being, rather than the center of his existence which she had become.

Onise turned his face to the wind and the snow, beating against his face. He awaited all the beneficence and peace they had to offer him. He thought that if he could make his forehead freeze, his blood would calm down and stop flowing so violently in his veins. He imagined that his heart would resume beating at its normal rate and his life would continue on its slow, boring, unremarkable path. But he was wrong. Dzidzia's tender face hovered before Onise, imprinting itself on his heart forever. He embraced the image as a mother cradles her firstborn child, and his hands passed over her hair as gently as the wind when it caresses a cocoon swaying from a branch, a breeze entrusted by nature to change the caterpillar into a butterfly.

Onise swore to himself not to look at or talk to Dzidzia. He was afraid of himself and knew what would happen if he tried to express his love openly. Not only was Onise afraid of speaking to Dzidzia; he was afraid even of moving or breathing, terrified of destroying by a single breath the thread of sanity that kept his body and psyche whole.

Dzidzia sat by Onise's side immersed in thought, afraid to interrupt the silence with a misplaced word. Who could have said what was going on inside her heart?

Who could have understood the waves that rolled inside her? What was haunting her? What picture was standing before her eyes to torture her?

If someone were to penetrate inside her secret thoughts at that moment, they would have seen the abyss of Dzidzia's heart open up before them, and they would have emerged from this abyss empty-handed, unenlightened, and discouraged. Dzidzia was clothed only in a thin *akaluxi*, with a shawl thrown on top to cover its bareness. Such tatters barely protected her from the wind and the shards of ice. She began to freeze, but she didn't say anything though the cold tore into her flesh and bones, filling her with grief.

Onise was so consumed by his own suffering that he failed to notice that Dzidzia was freezing. The *temi* had entrusted him with the task of looking after her. The defense of Dzidzia's honor and chastity had thereby become his duty. The mountaineers say, "even a wolf honors his word," and Onise had given his word to protect Dzidzia. At that moment, Onise was tempted by a desire which sucked the marrow out of his bones. His body grinded ruthlessly at his heart and made it impossible for him to carry out his duty with a peaceful conscience.

The draft, snow, and ice began to take their toll: Dzidzia started trembling. When Onise saw her body shaking, he felt as though he had been stung by a snake. He finally realized that she was trembling because of the rags she was wearing. Dzidzia, his holy-of-holies, the person to whom he addressed all his prayers and toward whom all his desires streamed, was in need! He had been so absorbed by his desire for her that he failed to notice her suffering.

A single turn of the head, a single glance, even a barely perceptible touch, were enough to release the trigger, for the gunpowder to explode, to set Onise's entire body on fire.

"My God! Dzidzia, what have I done? You're frozen to death and I didn't even notice!" Onise said in a shaking voice.

"Don't worry, dear Onise. I'm fine," Dzidzia said, trembling.

"How can you tell me not to worry? If you get sick, what would I do?" With these words, Onise took off Dzidzia's wet shawl and threw it on the sleigh, then raised the edge of his *nabadi* and wrapped it tightly around her. He pressed Dzidzia's trembling body against his chest to keep her warm. The closer her body was to his, the more excited and troubled he became. He stood up in a vain attempt to repress his exaltation. The bitter bliss of being alone together with his beloved made his body quake. Onise had forgot all about his duty to protect his best friend's bride and treat her like a sister. With every movement, with every touch and embrace, he forgot who he was and what he was doing sitting alone in a sleigh with his beloved. In spite of the cold, Dzidzia sat motionless and silent. She did not seem to have noticed Onise's agitation. Whether out of pity, fear, or because she felt his agitation, Dzidzia did not resist his advances.

A single feeling whispered sweetly into his ear: there is no happiness in the world greater than what you feel by Dzidzia's side right now, it said. He had no time, no energy to spare for the judgments of others. No matter how hard he tried, he could not be swayed by their cautions. He bent his head toward her face, burning already from the heat of his breath. He whispered into her ears the sweet words of love that only a sincere heart can utter. In all his earnestness, he could no longer speak of anything other than love.

"You're still freezing, Dzidzia! You're freezing, my angel! Let me make you warm." Onise said, as he wrapped his *nabadi* more tightly around his beloved. His voice trembled with the double-meaning of everything he said. Anyone who could have looked at him at that moment would have seen fire burning inside his heart. A new, wild love was beginning to dominate his soul.

Dzidzia rested on Onise's chest, as motionless as a trapped rabbit. She was still young, with no experience of the world. The only way she knew to respond to this unforeseen situation was by trembling. Until this moment, she had acted with restraint, had kept her feelings locked inside, but now, when Onise bent his head against hers, when his sporadic breaths hovered over the skin of her neck, the thread on which Dzidzia's sanity depended was cut. Dzidzia could no longer suppress her feelings. She looked up shyly and cast her grateful eyes toward Onise.

They were overcome with the same feeling, the same sensations, the same desires. An invisible power attracted them to each other. One minute passed, and then even they didn't know what drew their lips together.

VI.

God only knows how long the lovers would have continued caressing each other, if an unexpected event had not interrupted them. One of the groom's guests, hoping to warm himself with a shot of vodka, pulled his horse to a stop and waited for the sleigh carrying Onise, Dzidzia, and a sack of liquor, to pass by.

When the sleigh approached, the guest noticed that Onise, presumably because of the cold, had covered himself in his *nabadi*. The mountaineer did not like to see this kind of behavior from his fellow villager. He believed that a man should not reveal his weak side to a woman. According to mountaineer traditions, such behavior was so shameful and degrading, that it impugned the dignity and reputation of the entire village, and not only of the coward himself.

The guest hit Onise with his whip in a joking manner, but sharply enough to startle him:

"What do you think you're doing, my friend?" He yelled at Onise. "Have you lost your mind?"

Onise looked up in confusion. His first thought was that his brief spell of ecstasy had been ruined. But why? That was a question he could not answer. Onise only felt this for a second. He soon regained his consciousness and understood the true, bitter reality of the situation he was in. Not only were the fleeting moments of pleasure lost forever; lost as well was any hope of peace for himself in the future. Cold sweat poured from his face. Only a second earlier, he had been consumed by a single passion. He obeyed its demands heedlessly and sacrificed himself to that feeling. He had forgotten everything: his duty and responsibility before Dzidzia and his community, the rules and customs of his people. He had yielded to the trembling of his heart. It had been hard to resist its prompting once he saw that his caresses were well received by Dzidzia. Now that he had been deprived of the bliss of unconscious passion, Onise began to assess the damage.

Onise understood only now, when it was too late, that his desire to possess Dzidzia could never be fulfilled. Sparks of regret burned inside his head: "So all that trembling was in vain, all this restlessness inside my heart for nothing? Did Dzidzia and I embrace each other only to forget about our love now that we have to return to reality?" Such questions poured into his mind one after the other. Only one possible answer droned monotonously inside his brain: "Everything happened in vain. Your bliss belongs to the past."

"What happened, my friend?" the groom's guest asked. "Are you drunk?"

Onise gazed aimlessly in the direction of the speaker, though the face of his interlocutor's face did not register on his consciousness.

"What's that? What did you say?" asked Onise.

"I said, what are you doing? Are you sick? What's wrong?"

"By God, I don't know what went wrong," Onise said. "I'm not feeling well."

The guest approached closer to the sleigh, bent his head, and stared directly into Onise's face. Onise turned his head away from the guest's eyes and said angrily:

"What are you looking at me for? What do you want from me?"

"Nothing," the guest said in surprise and added, "I just wanted to see whether your face was red. I thought you might have a fever."

"What on earth do you expect to see on a night like this?" Onise said in an irritated tone. After a moment of silence, he added, "Maybe I do have a fever. My head hurts. I feel dizzy."

The guest continued to stare at Onise in disbelief. He looked as though he wanted to say something, but he didn't know what to say, so he curled his lips inward, struck his horse with his whip and galloped off into the cold, black distance. His conversation with Onise must have affected him strangely, because he had forgotten to take the vodka, for which he had stopped his horse in the first place, from the sleigh.

Several moments of silence passed. Both Onise and Dzidzia were absorbed in their thoughts, and an awkward silence fell between them. Suddenly, the wind carried to them a voice singing far away:

> Dance to your heart's fill.
> Sing like a *chianuri*.
> Never covet your neighbor's wife.
> She is one of your kin.

These words touched Onise's heart. The singing approached closer; Gugua's friends stopped and began their celebration. Soon afterward, the horsemen appeared. The young guests joked with each other and with Onise, but, when the man who had come in search of vodka told them that Onise was feeling sick and in no mood for joking, they left him alone. The guests suddenly stopped rejoicing and stood silently by the sleigh. An ominous silence ensued. Thin icy layers of snow blew incessantly from the south and covered the travelers' *nabadis* in white.

Thus they traveled silently, accompanied by Onise, the best man of the wedding, his gloomy heart locked tight, and the bewildered bride, who had experienced love for the first time in her life. She had tasted its sweetness and no longer knew what the future held in store for her.

Points of light twinkled in the thick fog. Soon, the vague outlines of homes were visible in the distance. At last the entire village could be seen. Only Onise sat with his head cast down. Consumed by bitter thoughts, he couldn't see anything except the chaos in his own mind.

Onise's indifference struck Gugua's friends as strange and uncalled for. So one youth shouted and fired his gun, while a second rushed toward the village hollering the good news, even though this was, according to tradition, Onise's job. But the merrymakers were too absorbed with their joy to mind that.

Onise soon recovered from his temporary lapse of consciousness but he was not able to join in the celebration. He knew that when they arrived in Gugua's village, he would lose his beloved forever. Losing Dzidzia meant losing his mind and therefore his sanity. He knew that neither he nor Dzidzia would have the power or the will to violate the traditions of their people.

VII.

The crowd entered the village and approached a chapel, in front of which stood a respectable-looking old man, with hair the color of snow. He greeted the guests. From the first glance, the deep lines on his kind face induced a feeling of respect. His eyes, wise but merciless, commanded the viewer's attention.

With an imperious expression on his face, Gocha, the elder of Xevi, father of his people, awaited the guests' arrival. According to the law of the mountains, he was to be the first to bless the bride and groom. With paternal condescension, he stood at attention, wishing them happiness. As Onise watched his father, to whom the entire region bowed, whose every request was fulfilled without delay, the color drained from his face, and his mouth became parched.

The sleigh finally came to a stop, but Onise was so confused that he couldn't manage to extract himself from it. His father shouted at him:

"Get out! What are you waiting for?"

Onise jumped to attention, flustered and unable to explain what he was doing. He stood petrified, as the crowd buzzed around him like bees.

Dzidzia was escorted out of the sleigh and toward Gocha, who took off his hat, called upon God and said:

"May God bless you!" He took her hand and added. "Poor girl, all frozen and trembling."

As he spoke, Gocha extended a second hand, and began to rub her fragile hands to warm them. Then he removed one hand and reached over to Gugua, standing by his side, and placed Dzidzia's hands on the groom's.

"May God unite that which man is powerless to divide!" the old man said sternly.

At these words, Dzidzia gasped and trembled even more intensely than before. Onise suddenly felt dizzy. His body began rocking back and forth. A man standing nearby grabbed hold of his arm to keep him from falling. The crowd joyously sang "Zhvaruli" as the bride and groom entered the chapel, where a priest dressed in a cassock was waiting.

Gocha turned again to his son. "What's wrong?" he asked, observing him with suspicious eyes.

"Nothing," Onise answered laconically. He bent his head. He couldn't endure the feeling of his father staring at him.

"How can you say nothing when you look more dead than alive? You can barely stand on your feet!"

"I'm not feeling well," Onise said apologetically.

"You're not feeling well?" his father repeated and stared more closely at his son. "So why are you here? Go and lie down. We'll find another best man."

One of Gugua's relatives had overheard the entire exchange between father and son. He implored Onise not to leave Gugua alone. Onise knew he would not be able to endure watching anymore. So he turned away and set off for his home. When he arrived he dropped immediately into bed. His consciousness was enveloped by the blackness of the night.

Gocha stayed in the chapel and watched the veiled bride, who trembled during the entire ceremony.

Several men who had been standing near by turned to Gocha, and, their hearts full of pity, said "Poor girl! How cold she is!"

Instead of answering, Gocha wiped his hand across his forehead and furrowed his brows.

The marriage was carried out according to tradition. Another youth was brought in to replace Onise as best man. Everything was ready. The priest turned to the groom and asked him if he was marrying the bride against his will or whether he was acting in accordance with his wishes. Gugua smiled, blushed, and signaled his agreement to the marriage by nodding his head. Then the priest turned to Dzidzia with the same question. In contrast to Gugua, the only sign of life Dzidzia emitted was a barely perceptible breathing which made her shoulders rise and fall.

Instead of answering, Dzidzia bent her head. A group of gossipy ladies by Dzidzia's side, who made a habit out of speaking for others, answered for her:

"Of course she wants to! Why do you need to ask? If she didn't want to, why would she be here?" They repeated one after another. Dzidzia stood by, utterly silent.

"So you're marrying this man according to your will?" the priest repeated.

"Yes, she's marrying according to her will, my dear priest! No one forced her to come here!" The gossipy ladies repeated. The priest, satisfied with their assurances, began to fulfill the seventh sacrament.

VIII.

The marriage ceremony passed joyfully as always. Gugua's friends made merry with the gossipy women. They had long looked forward to this opportunity for celebrating, and had no intention of letting the chance to laugh pass them by, though there was no real reason to rejoice in the goings-on.

Only Dzidzia the bride stood motionless and mute as a rock. Gocha's stoic face sparkled with a ray of inner light. His prayers had taken over his consciousness and he pled piously for the newlyweds' happiness.

As the *beri* of Xevi, Gocha was the father of his people, and therefore he was always present on holy days such as marriage to pray for his children. Along with this, he believed that he was chosen by his people and by God, because, among the customs of his people it was an article of faith that "the voice of God is the voice of the people." This belief had penetrated his flesh and blood. Gocha was certain that his earnest, sincere plea to God Almighty would be heard, and this faith gave him hope during his prayer and made him feel like the true and just leader of his people.

Gocha's face was marked by a wisdom attained over decades of experience. You could tell by looking at him that he was a humane, honest, and perceptive man. The expression and color on his face changed according to what was on his mind. From time to time, a mysterious sadness hung over his brows and accentuated the wrinkles on his face, but the gloom soon passed like a cloud, and he would redirect his pious eyes toward the sky and

the powerful rays of victory would illumine his face
once again.

With his intuitive sense of the rhythms of his son's
inner life, it was clear to Gocha that disaster was approaching. It was sufficient for him to see his son once
to know that sickness was not what was troubling him;
Onise was aching with another kind of sorrow. But what
exactly the problem was, the old man couldn't say,
though the air was saturated with danger and the hairs
on his arm stood on end.

When the marriage ceremony finished, the newlyweds were escorted into their new home. They circled
the hearth in the center of the room. Several people
moved aside to make room for Dzidzia. Then everyone
sat down to a supper, over which Gocha presided.

Gugua, a crown on his head, sat at the center of the
table with his friends surrounding him, as they toasted
his happiness. After the first round of toasts, the guests
continued drinking and singing, and passing the glasses
of wine around, and toasting each other. One of the old
men played the *panduri*. His fingers stroked the strings,
producing sounds resonating with sadness and narrating
the tales of heroes long ago.

The old man's singing broke through the chatter that
filled the room, and soon everyone was spellbound by
their visions of the heroes of days long ago. They listened to the tales of service and sacrifice to the country,
of courage and dignity, and the profound price which
everyone must pay to defend their country. Listening to
these stories of every man's and woman's duty to their
homeland, they heeded the message in these songs.

Then they returned to their toasts, to wine, and to improvising songs about love. The celebrations continued until dawn.

IX.

During this time of general rejoicing, as Gugua's friends came out and played in his house and danced on the ice without a care in the world, Onise lay on his bed with his head down. His soul was burdened, his head was on fire, and he could not lift his head from his pillow. The blood rushed to his eyes and made them sparkle like lighting. He felt dizzy as his temples reverberated. He felt as though a hammer was striking him. An incessant buzzing tormented his ears as the fire burned in his soul. He trembled violently in a vain attempt to break free of this weight.

Onise remained in this difficult position for a long time, until his body was frozen through, and cold sweat poured down his face. He turned over, sat up, and stared into the void that had become his life. His eyes and shoulders sank, and, with his lips half-opened, he stood still. Then he flung himself down again on the bed, and images of what had just transpired danced before his eyes once again. The pictures followed each other like a dream, each more stupefying than the next, rendering him numb to every feeling. There was nothing to link the pictures to each other, nothing to tie them together.

This oblivion passed soon enough. Onise jumped to his feet and cried out. Finally, he stopped wailing and rubbed his flaming eyes, which felt as though they were pricked by thorns, and said to himself: "This isn't possible! It wasn't supposed to happen this way!" Then he ran toward the door.

A voice suddenly stopped him in his tracks. Gocha appeared at the threshold, an illuminated candle in his hand. "Where are you going?" he asked.

"Gocha!" Onise backed away from the door in shock.

The old man fixed his eyes on his child's face, entered his house, and sat down.

"Take this. Hang it on the wall." Gocha gestured toward the candle, which Onise took from him and lay on the mantle of the fireplace.

"Where were you going?" the old man repeated, though this time in a calmer, less menacing voice.

"Nowhere," Onise mumbled in confusion.

"What kind of an answer is that?" Gocha furrowed his brows and stared at his son with suspicion.

"I wanted to go to the wedding," Onise said at last.

"What wedding? All that's left is a bunch of drunkards."

"The mountains are covered with snow and the animals have come down from the cliffs. I thought that I could find someone at the wedding to go hunting together with me."

Onise invented this lie on the spur of the moment. His father started at him silently and then demanded that he give an account of himself, but Onise did not wish to open his heart to his father.

"Boy, are you kidding me?"

"What do you mean? Why would I kid you?" Onise said in irritation. Why couldn't his father simply leave him alone?

"No one in their right mind goes hunting in this kind of snow! An avalanche will bury you somewhere and you'll never see the light of day again. Is that what you want?"

Onise didn't know what to say. True, it was dangerous and even pointless to go hunting in this kind of snow. He also knew that Xevisberi Gocha did not like to be deceived.

"Why?" Onise vainly attempted to correct his mistake. "There was a strong wind, and the snow has been blown off the slopes."

The old man watched his son in silence. After a few minutes, he said, "Don't lie to me, boy. Something else is bothering you."

"What do you mean?" Onise asked, feigning incomprehension.

"I don't know and I won't ask." Gocha said firmly, and then added. "All I'll say to you is this: Do you remember your ancestors?"

Onise turned in surprise toward his father and looked into his eyes. "Yes, I remember my ancestors."

"Good." Gocha said. "Don't you ever forget them. Remember who your ancestors are, and don't you ever make a fool of yourself."

Onise bent his head in guilt and his cheeks turned red from shame.

"Then go," the old man said. "Go wherever you want. "But don't you ever forget my words. Remember your ancestors and remember that man was created to suffer."

He took the candle down from the wall and escorted Onise to the porch. He stopped and stared at his son as though he wanted to say something but couldn't find the words. Then he turned around and returned inside.

Onise stood motionless, unable to make sense of what had happened. He knew that his father had guessed he was in trouble, but he didn't know how deeply his father perceived his desperation. One thing was certain: if his son had a problem, that was a risk for Gocha's reputation, too.

His father had told him to remember who his ancestors were, reminding him with these words of the duty which unites every mountaineer to his entire family, and which can be either a source of shame or of pride, depending on how well the duty is honored. Even if his father had not chastised him, Onise would have felt his duty toward his people all the same. He repented his reckless behavior and swore to eradicate the feelings that had arisen in his heart. Emboldened by these reflections, Onise said out loud: "I'll go to the wedding all the same. I have a beard. I'm a man. I have a hat to cover my head, and I can control my heart."

Together with these words, he turned toward the staircase, jumped down several steps, and entered his best friend's house, where the dancing and singing had not yet stopped, in spite of the fact that it was already dawn. Everyone greeted Onise joyfully, and he began to sing and dance with the intensity of a person who has gone insane.

X.

Dzidzia and Gugua passed the first days of marriage in feasts and celebrations. In keeping with tradition, the bride was escorted by the village girls to the spring to collect water, where the girls treated her to a pie they had baked specially for her and sang a song in which the newly wedded bride addresses the best man who has brought her to her groom:

> My best man
> Hang the bucket
> On my shoulder

Finally, after many days of celebration, the wedding ended. Life once again assumed its familiar face.

Dzidzia turned out to be a wonderful, attentive wife. She fulfilled all her tasks diligently. She never complained. She never objected to her husband's orders. Her sisters-in-law, so accustomed to insulting and lording it over new members of the family, regarded Dzidzia as their real sister as soon as she entered the household.

Gugua adored his wife. He never returned home from work without bringing with him a small gift for her, whether a red apple or a piece of *churchelo*. He kissed his wife rapturously every evening. Given all the attention lavished on her, no one could understand what made Dzidzia so quiet, why she constantly sought to be alone, why she never smiled, and why her lips were drained of blood.

Everyone tried to cheer her up. She was given more freedom than the other sisters-in-law of that region. The family took her with them to religious celebrations and funerals, where those who had been separated for years could meet and catch up on old times.

But Dzidzia remained as quiet as ever, her heart as closed to the world as it had always been since the day she was married. She had everything a wife could wish for: food, drink, clothes. She never lacked for care, protection, and even love, but for some reason she began to languish, and became apathetic and exhausted.

At first, her new family tried to understand her, to figure out what made this gentle, good-natured woman so sad, but they soon gave up hope. They discovered that the depths of Dzidzia's heart could not be penetrated by anyone and decided that it was her nature to be so sad.

After the wedding, Onise went to Pshavi, a region bordering on Xevi, where his uncles on his mother's side lived. He intended to go hunting, to pasture sheep, and to kill the pain that burned inside him. But whenever he set his eyes on the mountains that should have divided him from his grief, Dzidzia's face illuminated his heart and the blissful misery of her presence made him moan with grief. The sky, the clouds, the moon, and nature itself seemed beautiful to Onise only insofar as they reflected Dzidzia's face, only insofar as they reminded him what it felt like to touch his beloved's skin.

XI.

The dark and gloomy winter soon passed, and along with it disappeared the bullet-colored clouds darkening the canyons and mountain tops that had brought grief to anyone who looked at them. The cold north winds no longer swept through the mountains with their shrill whistle, casting the icy snow upon the soft ground, which sucked up its moisture, crumbling the ice into dust, and scattering it into the air.

Nature's rebirth was underway: the restless drone of the wind alternated with a light breeze. The sun warmed the earth as vegetation spread over its surface. The grass rose, shedding the shroud of snow that covered the soil. Snow melted and flooded the ravines. The Caucasus, freed at last from the unpleasant weight of winter, shook their manes, revealing green velvet layers petrified beneath the sad layers of ice. The flowers awoke, swaying back and forth. They were playing a game of courtship and trying to seduce each other. The sun's rays relished the flowers' beauty, but the coy flowers rejected their advances. Only the diligent worker bees were able to suck the sweet nectar from the flowers, as their furry, gentle legs rubbed against the pollen.

Pearls of morning dew cooled the green leaves, heated by the sun. The lamentation and chirping of the birds resonated softly in the air; paradise, they knew, was not far away. They called to their friends, inviting them to participate in the rebirth of nature. Their hearts beat gleefully and their wings flapped wildly as they swung from the branches.

Onise watched nature rejoice, though spring had not yet visited his heart. Instead, inside his soul, a black cloud cast a dark shadow over everything that should have been green. Sweetness filled the air, but the only emotion it stirred in him was sadness.

He gasped and groaned. He couldn't escape the pain in his soul and wandered the hills and plains like a wounded lion. He was so full of grief that he decided to return home. He wanted to hear the whispering of the crystal-clear waters. No matter how delicious the waters of other lands were, nothing could compare to the water of his homeland. He ran from cliff to cliff like an enraged tiger and jumped into the Tergi River. Onise wanted to see once again those places which had given him so much joy and pain, but he couldn't make up his mind to start the journey back home. He was afraid. What if his strength failed him? He remembered his father's words—"Remember who your ancestors are. Don't you ever make a fool of yourself."—and he couldn't make up his mind what to do.

Onise had initially hoped to kill his feelings for Dzidzia by traveling far away from her. With that hope in mind, he wooed the beautiful girls of Tusheti. He had hoped to be satiated by their caresses, but as soon as he opened his mouth to compliment them on their beauty, Dzidzia's face rose before his eyes. She gazed at him with a smile so entrancing that it drove him crazy with desire and burst open the floodgates of his passion. It was as though the words were written on her face: "You try to free yourself from me, but you're my slave. You'll never escape my grasp." Onise attended to these words, which repeated themselves in his brain, and his be-loved's face became demonic, her wicked grin enslaving him to the fantasy of a love he'd never experience but always long for.

Onise passed these months in despair. He felt that he'd squandered his youth on a passion that would never be consummated. His life became saturated by the consciousness of his own insufficiency. All his thoughts pointed in one direction. If he was to live and maintain his sanity, he would have to banish love from his life.

XII.

One day, at the foot of one of the mountains in the Arxoti chain, where the Tushetians kept their sheep, the shepherds feasted together on a sheep they had sacri-ficed to God. Several mountaineers from Xevi formed part of this group. They shared their sheep with the Tu-shetians during the pasturing season. The meat was al-ready cooked, and they were in the process of sitting down around the table according to their ages. Half of them had already sat down, when a man appeared on the slope's horizon, a gun slung over his back and the bottom edges of his *choxa* folded upward. He raced forward, his hat in his hand, wiping the sweat that poured down from his face.

It appeared that the messenger had come on urgent business. He raced toward the shepherds, who stood motionless, observing him closely. They were rarely vis-ited by people from other parts of the world. Every traveler who passed through came with news. They hoped to get news of their native village and family, and waited for the newcomer with their hearts beating hard, wishing that he would run faster. They asked each other: "Who could it be? Why is he in such a hurry to reach us?"

The sun was setting in the direction the messenger had come from. Its rays streamed directly into the shepherd's faces. They shielded their eyes with their hands and continued to watch and wait. Onise was among this group. The impatience shared by everyone was etched in particular relief on his face. He rushed down the mountain to meet the messenger before the others.

The stranger was still far away. As he rushed toward the group, he descended into a small canyon that curved over a river. Onise stared with agitation at the spot from which the stranger had disappeared. At long last, the traveler appeared again. Onise screamed with joy and surged toward him like a falcon. He had recognized in the messenger's face a man whom he knew from Xevi, one of his childhood friends.

"Peace be with you, Data!" Onise screamed, still far away from the traveler.

"May God grant you peace, Onise." The messenger yelled back.

They approached each other at the same rate, and finally reached each other and embraced. They stood side by side, silently. Onise could not utter all that was in his heart. The thousand questions he wanted to ask all vied for expression. But, waiting for his friend to speak first, he didn't say anything.

At first, Onise took Data's strange silence for a joke. Data continued staring without uttering a word. The traces of joy which the sight of an old friend had prompted disappeared from his face. Onise feared that some tragedy must have struck Xevi, something so awful that it prevented Data from moving his mouth.

As he stared back at his friend, the color drained from Onise's face.

"Tell me, what happened? What's going on?" Onise implored, his voice trembling. He felt like he was going to fall and pushed his hands forward to steady himself.

"Let's go inside and I'll tell you," the messenger answered. "I'll tell everyone."

Onise could only think of one thing. His mind had room for one face only. Every thought and emotion in his heart related to Dzidzia and therefore he felt convinced that the messenger had arrived for the sole purpose of telling him about Dzidzia. Had something happened to her? He thought that the messenger was afraid of telling him the truth. Onise forgot that there was no way Data could know the trepidation in his heart; his love for his best friend's wife was a secret. Data therefore had no reason to pity his friend or to fear speaking the truth. For Onise, however, only one problem existed. There was only one question in the world worth asking. His mind was obsessed with this single issue. Nothing else mattered.

"Tell me the truth, Data. Don't hide it from me." Onise said. "What's the point in staring at the animal you're about to sacrifice to God, when it's already on the slaughtering block?"

Data looked at Onise and noticed that he had the countenance of a corpse. He surmised that Onise was worried that something had happened to his father or another member of his family.

"Why are you so worried?" Data asked. "All your family is healthy and well."

"Don't you lie to me, by God!" Onise warned his friend.

"Onise, I swear by God and his angels that I'm not lying."

The conversation stopped. Data turned toward the shepherds and Onise followed, as if by instinct.

"Data, if everything's fine, then why do you refuse to tell me what's going on?" Onise inquired, his heart full of suspicion.

"Your family couldn't be safer. I swear nothing is wrong!"

"Wait a second!" Onise began, and he couldn't finish what he had to say. He wanted to ask about Dzidzia, but didn't dare pronounce her name. Data stood silently, waiting for Onise to continue speaking.

"What's the matter?" Data asked at last.

"So . . . my father's ok?" Onise couldn't think of anything else to say. Data stared at his friend, surprised by his inarticulateness.

"Are you crazy or what, Onise?"

"Tell me! Tell me everything!" Onise said in a voice so full of desperation that anyone who heard him speak would have pitied him, without knowing why.

"Gocha is fine. Your uncles are doing well, too, thank God. All your relations, everyone, is doing great.

They have everything they need, and couldn't ask for more."

"So what's wrong?"

"Nugzar Eristavi wants to makes us into slaves. That's why I came to see you."

"What?" Onise couldn't believe what he was hearing.

"If we don't surrender, he said he'll kill us all."

"We'll die in battle before we give in." Onise furrowed his brows. "He'll never make slaves of us."

The other shepherds arrived and joined in on the conversation.

"Of course we're ready to defend our freedom" said one shepherd. "But everyone knows how stubborn Nugzar is. Once he makes a threat, he'll carry it out to the end. This battle won't end without the shedding of blood."

"So what are the people of Xevi going to do?" everyone asked together.

"They're getting ready," Data answered, "and they won't give in without a fight. Young men are preparing for battle everywhere in these mountains. They're traveling to inform all the shepherds of the news, and they sent me here to you. Nugzar has gathered all of Mtiuleti on his side. The Ossetians are also standing by supporting him, ready to attack us. They've already reached the Trusso Ravine."

"Let's go! Let's go!" several men yelled. They hoisted their weapons high in the air, ready to declare war.

"What do the Ossetians want?" Onise asked. For the first time since the conversation began, Dzidzia's face no longer floated before Onise's eyes.

"The Ossetians say they want to be mediators and help us out, but in reality they spoil everything. They can't do anything to us by themselves, so they now rely on Nugzar, their only hope."

"Men," Onise addressed the shepherds, "we have no time to spare. Let's go! We'll find out what we need to know when we get there."

"Let's go! Let's go!" the shepherds answered in unison. They hurried to collect their possessions and weapons before it was too late.

XIII.

The day was beginning to break. A thick layer of fog floated over the Tergi River, covering the entire area and the village. In several places, the mountain tips ripped through the mist; they seemed to be standing in the air without support from below. The sun's rays penetrated the blue sky and painted it red. The stars felt the approach of day and their weak twinkling became even dimmer. Old Elbrus gazed down below with pride at Sameba, a mountain named after the ancient Church of the Holy Trinity, which had been erected on its slope and preserved throughout many centuries. The edifice that remained, surrounded by green flowers, offered but a dim memory of the glorious days of long ago. Beneath the church stood the same fog, seeking with its dense power to liberate the past from its earthly chains.

From the heights of Sameba, the ground below seemed bathed in beauty. The world was deep asleep and filled with a silent sadness. The usually restless wind held its breath, no longer caressing the leaves. Only on rare occasions would rocks dislodged by startled mountain goats roll down the slopes and break the silence that filled the air. The avalanche of falling rocks united with the waterfall's melody as it cascaded down the mountains, singing its lullaby to sleeping nature.

All of a sudden, a high-pitched sound interrupted this idyllic scene. A restless bird's song filled the air for several minutes, as she felt the approach of dawn or perhaps detected the sleeping shadow of her male companion.

The sun's flames painted Mount Elbrus a fiery red, its rays glistening on the surface of the crystal snow like a golden tiara. A partridge called on his sweetheart to join in the celebration; he didn't want to experience nature's bliss alone. The sweet rebirth of nature was not merely a matter of sound. Mountain goats, worn out by long nights of roaming the forest and mountain tops, struggled to move forward, as the white, glistening snow called upon nature to play. The pleasant scents stirred the goats to dizziness and enveloped them in a bliss they could only free themselves from by shaking their heads.

Not far away, in the forest, a blackbird chirped in ecstasy over nature's bliss. A bell resounded from somewhere in the church. A mild breeze scattered the sound through the mountains. The bell resounded again, then another time. Finally, it turned into a steady appeal. Apparently, the guards of the temple had awoken and were calling the villagers to assemble.

The morning breeze blew softly, and, with the help of the sun's rays, shook and stirred the mist, which, like a lover caught unawares by the passage of time, disappeared at the approach of dawn and sought a peaceful refuge behind the mountains. The ravine appeared through the fog as the foamy, wild Tergi River flowed like a rabid beast along its spine. Everywhere, people were moving back and forth and the villages were coming to life. People gathered in groups at the entrance to every village. In the middle of every group, at the center of every village, stood a flag, hoisted high, calmly swaying in the breeze.

The bell rang incessantly from the Church of the Holy Trinity. Suddenly, the mass of people shook, the men took off their hats and began singing in a low bass note, a song which they called "Gergetul." Their voices emanated through the mountains like thunder. The flag bearers led the procession; behind them followed the remaining villagers, who would jump into fire and die in battle if they had to protect their flag, this symbol of their honor and dignity.

Everyone made their way toward the Church of the Holy Trinity. They raced to the temple where the *temi* was supposed to gather in preparation for a meeting that was to determine the fate of Xevi. Once a decision had been taken by the *temi*, everyone without exception was expected to blindly obey its orders.

Xevisberi Gocha and his assistants waited for the meeting to begin. During the past two weeks, they had been fasting and praying, in pursuit of spiritual purification, to make themselves worthy of touching the flag.

Touching the flag was not a light matter for those entrusted with this honor. A decision taken in front of a flag such as this one could never be revoked. Every Moxeve would chose death, alienation from their mothers, brothers, and even from their beloveds, rather than renege on an oath taken before Xevi's most sacred symbol. A word uttered in the presence of the *temi* could never be denied.

Nor was the business that had caused the *temi* to gather on this day a joking matter. The mountaineers, who valued their freedom more than anything else, were now threatened with enslavement. Everyone, even their neighbors with whom they had formerly had good relations, had sworn to wage war against them. The ravenous Nugzar had said he would attack their villages and rip his prey to pieces like a lion. Mtiuleti was already under his rule, but the mere subjugation of this small region could never satisfy the imperial passions of a man like Nugzar Eristavi. He couldn't endure the thought that any of his neighbors were free. Nugzar thirsted for subjugation and was prepared to do anything to achieve his aim, even if he had to shed his brother's blood.

The Moxeves understood how serious this situation was and determined to meet the enemy with dignity and honor.

XIV.

The Church of the Holy Trinity stands on the top of one of Elbrus's slopes, at the end of the mountain range that cuts into the Tergi River. At the foot of this ravine stands the village of Gergeti. The church has a bell tower and a meeting hall, both hewn from stone. Nature has encircled the slope with powerful cliffs. In a few places, human hands have fortified this stronghold.

There is no rock near by the village out of which the temple was chiseled. The water flows into the ravine at a considerable distance. One small path leads to this temple, which a man can ascend only with difficulty. Those who ascend these steps make their way forward in surprise, as they ask themselves: Where did they bring the materials for this wonderful edifice, and how did they carry the stones here?

Fig. 8. Cminda Sameba near Mount Qazbeg.

The building is testimony to the great deeds that humans are capable of when they work together. A marble stone was lodged in a corner of the temple, on which were inscribed words that neither rain nor wind have been able to erase: "Xari-Loma . . . Tevdore the shepherd." The names were those whose good deeds made possible the building of this monument to Xevi's glorious past.

The villagers spread over the mountain and gathered in the fields. A cross and then a large flag was hoisted over the walls surrounding the temple. Everyone fell to their knees and began praying to the defenders of Xevi in times long past.

A bare-headed man appeared on the edge of the slope, his mane of hair and long beard unfurled and white. He stood like an ancient prophet, his white linen shirt tied to his body with a simple rope. Gocha's lively but stern face, full of cares and troubles, won over every heart and lured them to obedience. Flag bearers dressed in white *choxas* took the local flags of every village from the people and hoisted them around the big flag of Xevi. Everyone was quiet; even the wind calmed down, as though it too understood that the fate of the Moxeve people was to be determined that day. The old man shook the flag. The general silence was interrupted by the twinkling of bells. Shudders raced through the veins of the kneeling masses.

"They're blessing the flag! Gocha is saying a prayer!" people began whispering, and their voices traveled like a breeze through the crowd.

Gocha shook the flag again. Again the bells twinkled. He made the sign of the cross and blessed the people, the holy words soft and sweet on his lips. After the general prayer, Gocha read a prayer in honor of Xevi's heroes, those men who didn't spare themselves for the well-being of their people. He blessed those who rushed forward first to expel the enemy and who stood with their weapons cocked. He ended with an appeal to God, that he would not cast his eye away from Xevi and that he would protect his children forever.

During the blessing ceremony, in the intervals between Gocha's speech, exclamations of approval rushed through the crowd: "Amen! Amen! God bless you!" The mountains resonated with the bass tones of the male choir. Then the voices dissipated into the air.

When Gocha finished his prayer, he announced to the crowd the news concerning Nugzar Eristavi's plans to attack. The people, who had been quiet until now, suddenly became agitated.

"Be quiet!" Gocha insisted in a loud voice several times. Then he resumed his speech: "God is great and generous! He'll never abandon the fruit of his hands. Neither will he forget us. What does Nugzar want from us? Why does he seek to destroy our family? We honor the king of Georgia. May the life of any Moxeve be darkened forever who pities his child and refuses to sacrifice himself for the sake of his people. We were born to serve our brothers, and that's the way it should be. What is a brother worth who refuses to sacrifice himself in a time of need? Nugzar has set his voracious eyes toward us. He wants to instigate hatred between two peaceful neighbors, to make the Mtiuletians and the Moxeves kill each other, so he can rule over us all the better. What do you say to this, my people? A battle against Nugzar will not be easily won. The Mtiuletians have forgotten the meaning of brotherhood, and they are preparing to attack us. Are we going to surrender?"

A wave of agitation passed through the crowd. Their voice merged into a single word, which trembled in the air, relentlessly repeating itself: "No! No! No!"

Suddenly, a young man came out onto the field, in front of where the people were standing. He motioned to everyone to be silent, and said, "Gocha! Why do you have to even ask us? Moxeves have not forgotten the meaning of brotherhood, and, by God, we only wish the best for our neighbors and are willing to sacrifice everything for their sake. Let anyone die who refuses to support us. Let the man be shamed forever who betrays his neighbors. Any Moxeve who chooses slavery is doomed to die! Nugzar has conquered others and now he flatters himself that it will be easy to subjugate us. The Mtiuletians don't remember the brotherhood we shared and are now coming to us as enemies. We're only born once, and we wish to die with our dignity intact. We'll perish by our own hands before we allow a foreign people to rule over us."

The people responded to this speech with a round of hurrahs. "We will die! We will die!" they shouted.

An old man made his way toward the boy who had just arrived onto the field, leaned on his walking stick, and said: "Onise! My God, you are your father's child through and through. You bear the mark of courage on your face. A brave man always chooses death over shame and will be buried alive before he goes back on his word. When a brave man takes a vow, it is always carried out. But the Mtiuletians are our brothers. Nugzar has lured them with his false promises. Let's try first to negotiate with them before we attack them. With the Ossetians, however, we don't need to be polite."

After the old man finished speaking, the people divided into two groups. One group supported a war against anyone and everyone, regardless of whether they were brothers or enemies, while the second group considered it a mistake to attack without first making attempts at negotiation. Both sides debated with each other incessantly without reaching an agreement.

Once again, the bells twinkled and a veil of silence fell over the crowd.

"People!" Gocha began. "We have no time to waste on fruitless debate. The enemy stands at our gates. Let the leaders of the *temi* come forward. Whether they're our friends or enemies, we must be prepared to meet them. Come forward, men of the *temi*!"

After Gocha finished speaking, the delegates chosen by the people emerged from the crowd, gathered into groups, and set off for the meeting hall in the Church of the Holy Trinity, where, under Gocha's leadership, the other leaders of the community were to determine the future of Xevi.

XV.

The leaders of the *temi* didn't need to talk for a long time, because everyone had decided already on freedom, even at the price of death. The commanders of the army were chosen, as well as the leaders, the artillerymen, and the negotiators, who were to be sent to negotiate with the Mtiuletians. In accordance with the established rules, Gocha assumed for himself the authority of issuing orders.

In keeping with tradition, after the discussion, Gocha dispatched the negotiators and ended the meeting. They had three days to prepare for battle. Then every man would come out onto the field and there they would block the enemy's path.

The crowd dispersed in all directions, everyone except for Gocha and the flag bearers, who remained behind to pray to God one last time and implore him to look after Xevi.

Onise was among those running back and forth. He hurried toward his village, where the bliss of seeing Dzidzia's face awaited him. Onise's friends pestered him with questions about the Tushetians and the Pshavs, but he had only one thing on his mind, which had nothing to do with Tushetia or Pshavi, and therefore he answered without paying attention to his words. Onise and his friends reached a field where the girls of Xevi were busy gathering blueberries and raspberries.

"Look, Onise!" one of his companions yelled to him. "The girls have spread like sheep over that valley." The speaker pointed toward the girls.

Onise turned his head to silence his annoying interlocutor, who kept him far away from his private thoughts. But as soon as his eyes took in the sight, his pulse quickened and he rubbed his hands across his forehead, already coated in sweat.

"What happened?" Onise's companion asked, surprised by the change in his friend's face.

"Nothing!" Onise said sharply, then added in a calmer voice, "Nothing at all. Just that these sharp rocks have ripped my shoes and cut my feet."

Onise limped toward a rock nearby, sat down, and began to unlace his shoes.

Onise's companion rushed toward him and tried to take over. "Don't trouble yourself. I'll take off your shoes for you."

"I don't want that, my friend. I want to take them off myself." Onise was at his wits end. He didn't know what else he could do to get this man to leave him alone.

"Have pity on me," the stranger began. "Please let me help you. Don't be stubborn like a little child. At least let me take them off you!" He extended his hands in Onise's direction.

Onise could no longer repress his irritation. "I told you, I'll take them off myself!" he yelled. Soon, however, he regained control of himself and added, "The sun has nearly set. Take care not to be late in getting home. I'm tired and want to rest."

Onise's companion looked toward the setting sun. Instead of replying, he shielded his eyes with his hat and made off for home.

Alone at last, Onise entered an enclave and hid there in such a way that passersby could not detect his presence, though he had a good view of everyone who passed him. From here, he could watch the Moxeve girls, and Dzidzia in particular, gather the berries.

Those villagers who had gathered by the Church of the Holy Trinity descended the slope and hurried home to prepare themselves for the day of battle.

Onise sat in his refuge and, with his heart beating fast, watched the girls collect the berries and improvise poems for each other. Only Dzidzia sat apart from the others. Her face was pale and sad, and she gathered the berries with her head hung low.

If you had looked at the girls from far away, you would have thought that Dzidzia did not belong to the group, that she had nothing in common with them. Onise stared at her, feeling sick himself. She was the beginning and the end of his being. He wanted to call her name, to say "Dzidzia, I am here. Come to me. You are my destiny. Only I can make you happy." But the words stuck in his throat. He didn't want Dzidzia's companions to find out about the secret movements of his heart. Nor did he wish to cast a stain on his beloved's reputation.

Unsuspectingly, the girls approached the place where Onise was hidden. As they drew close, Onise was overcome by trembling. Dzidzia's face shone more brilliantly with every step she took in his direction, and filled him with a mysterious power, which bound his heart and crippled his body. Like a magnet, this power pulled him in the direction of his beloved.

Suddenly, the girls turned and set off in the opposite direction. Onise almost screamed with joy, when he watched Dzidzia separate herself from the other girls and head in his direction. He breathed so hard that his heart began to palpitate, held captive as it was by Dzidzia's proximity.

Dzidzia emerged from the enclave, laid down her basket, and sat down by the rustling waters' edge. She cast her sad eyes toward the ground and fell into thought. Onise watched his beloved silently. He yearned to approach her, but a mysterious force took away his power over himself. He did not dare to breathe, for even the mildest movement of the air could attract attention, and startle the gentle creature seated nearby.

All of a sudden, Dzidzia moaned and her eyes filled with tears. A tear hung on her long black eyelashes like a pearl. It was followed by another, and then another, until Dzidzia was weeping, silently and incessantly.

Onise could not endure the suffering he saw Dzidzia was going through, and he approached her quietly.

"Dzidzia, why do you cry?" Onise whispered in a voice as gentle as the wind.

To Dzidzia, however, Onise's voice was so powerful that she managed to glance only once at him before her face recoiled in fear. She sat motionless as a stone, staring at Onise. Only her lips showed that she wanted to say something, but she could not produce the right sounds.

"Dzidzia, tell me. What do you want to say?" Onise said as he kneeled in front of Dzidzia. "What are you keeping from me? Have you forgotten that I'm your best man?"

Dzidzia trembled. The color returned to her face. Her eyes sparkled and her lips formed into a smile. She was so consumed by her emotions that she couldn't articulate her desires to herself. At last she reached out her hands toward Onise and said: "Onise, where did you come from?"

Onise crept closer to Dzidzia and rested by her side, half lying down, his head propped on his hands. As he stared at Dzidzia, his soul on fire, it seemed to him that the years of separation had not only not extinguished the flame of love in his heart but that, to the contrary, the flame burned all the more intensely on account of their separation, which spurred him to action now. His attempts to forget her had been in vain. One encounter with Dzidzia, one glance in her direction, was enough to make him forget everything but the name of his beloved.

"Dzidzia! Dzidzia!" Onise repeated, his voice trembling. He couldn't remember anything sweeter than the sounds of her name which his lips formed.

Dzidzia clearly felt the same as Onise, because the fear vanished from her face as she bent her fragile body toward Onise's chest.

Within a few seconds, the two lovers were staring at each other in awe. Their faces pressed against each other, as their souls merged into the breaths they shared. Suddenly, a violent wind ripped Dzidzia's scarf off her head. Her black curls fell down onto her shoulders and seduced Onise with their beauty. The sight of her raven locks was enough to open the floodgates of Onise's passions. His self-restraint abandoned him, and their lips became entwined.

Who knows how far their embraces would have gone, how long they would have spent making love, if the noise of the girls gathering berries had not cut short their blissful oblivion?

Dzidzia suddenly recalled the ties that bound her to Onise. Ever since the day of her wedding he had become the equivalent of her brother. He was supposed to protect her, but he could not get involved in any other way. She arched her eyebrows and wrinkled her face. Her skin acquired a lifeless white hue, oppressed by pain. Then she pushed Onise away and rose to her feet. She ran off in the direction of her friends. Onise remained in his place, confused and full of grief. He did not understand why Dzidzia had left him.

Dzidzia joined her friends who had approached the enclave, while Onise watched his beloved with a fast-beating heart. Dzidzia's lips had blossomed into roses for the first time since the wedding. The sparks of pleasure danced in her eyes while her long, beautiful, neck swayed like a gazelle's.

As Onise watched his beloved, one question repeated itself in his brain: "Why did she abandon me? Why didn't she say anything to me? Will I ever again feel her caresses?"

The girls moved away from the enclave. Onise stood to his feet and stretched his arms. His body was enlivened with a power, the like of which he had never felt before. Dzidzia loved him: the world was his possession.

XVI.

Where a road now travels from Georgia to the north, passes the village of Kobi, and then a field, it twists in three directions, and wraps around the polished stones like a belt. A proud tower rises over the cliff of Sion, and stands as a guard to the mountain, with enough power to make any enemy tremble. The place where the tower stands is the main entrance into Xevi. The

Narovani Mountain Pass is the only indirect route into Xevi. Nature has created in this spot an impenetrable sanctuary, with its own fields for pasturing the sheep, rivers and forests. In times past, this region was considered one of the safest places in all of Xevi, where the mountaineers could take refuge during times of war. There was a small field on top of the cliff, above which stood houses chiseled out of sharp, jagged rocks, fortifying the already strong sanctuary that nature had created.

This was the place where the people of Xevi had gathered in the past in order to restrain the bloody desires of the enemy.

Because Xevisberi Gocha required many people for the defense of Xevi, he issued the order that every able-bodied man and boy must appear on the field of battle. So that the women would not be left idle, and in order to involve them in the preparations for war, Gocha announced that they would bring milk, butter, and cheese to the army from the mountains where the sheep were milked. Regarding bread, however, everyone was instructed to get it from their own home. In such a way, food was distributed equally to everyone, though some of those who received food didn't have anything of their own to contribute to the common share.

A sufficient supply of bullets was brought in from the village of Xde, while others set about the task of making gunpowder. Ammonium was gathered from the caves, where it lay scattered like salt. Sulfur was added to it. The mixture was then placed on a fire of birch tree logs and branches.

The Moxeves thus prepared themselves for battle and strengthened their hideouts in the forest, to make sure that even if things did not go their way and they lost the battle, at least the enemy would pay a high price for their defeat.

One night, when it was so dark that a person could not see the fingers in front of his eyes, quiet rustlings of human voices echoed from the bottom floor of the fortress. A group of strangers approached the place where the path joined with the forest, when suddenly they heard several people speaking and were forced to stop.

"Who goes there? Stop if you value your life!"

Together with these words, the travelers felt the cold steel barrels of several guns pressed against their chests.

"Who are you?" the speaker repeated.

"We're from the Church of the Holy Trinity," was the answer. "We're your people."

"Where are you going?"

"We're on our way to see Xevisberi Gocha."

"Where did you come from?"

One of the travelers answered the question and then added, "Onise, is that you?"

"Yes, I'm Onise." He peered into the stranger's face. "Tolike! How could I not have recognized you? I'm so glad you've returned!"

"May God bless you!" the newcomer answered and asked, "Where is Gocha? I need to see him right away."

"Follow me," Onise said, and immediately they set off toward Gocha.

Tolike had been sent to the Mtiuletians as a negotiator. Every Moxeve awaited his return with a trembling heart. The Mtiuletians' answer would determine whether they would live in peace with each other or fight to the death. Like everyone else, Onise yearned to hear the results of the negotiations, but he did not want this secret news to fall into the wrong hands. So he remained silent.

Onise was barely conscious of his yearning to inquire about the fate of the negotiations. His silence, driven by instinct alone, proved the extent to which he valued his people's well-being and understood the necessity of holding his tongue.

The negotiators followed Onise in complete silence. All their lives they had been told that one superfluous word can bring irrevocable evil. Even if they had been chopped into a hundred pieces, they would have never leaked the secret with which they had been entrusted.

They made their way toward Gocha, who stood up to greet the visitors, escorted them into his bedroom, and seated them on a bedstead made of simple, sturdy wood.

Onise stood facing Gocha and the guests, awaiting his father's orders. His father did not delay for long.

"Boy, did you accompany the guests here?" Gocha asked his son.

"Yes."

"Good, then go now and look after your friends. Just be careful. If you let anyone slip away, the sun will rise on your grave."

"My God!" Onise said. "Don't I have a hat on my head? Am I not a man?" He bent his head, waved goodbye, and left the house.

"May God follow you wherever you go," one of the guests shouted to Onise as he left. Gocha remained silent, but his eyes were so full of love and his face radiated such pleasure when he heard his son's answer that it was obvious to everyone that for Gocha, the sun and the moon revolved around his son.

XVII.

Nugzar Eristavi did not sit idly while the Moxeves were preparing to meet the enemy. He too was attempting to increase his army in every possible way. He too was making plans for a surprise attack, and intended to break the Moxeves' stubborn will.

Nugzar was not satisfied to have the Ossetians and Mtiuletians fighting on his side; he wanted to have the Khandosxevians, Chartlians, and the Gudamaqrians on his side as well. He had sent messengers to these regions and every day waited impatiently for an answer. He was also waiting to hear back from the Lezgins in Dagestan, on whom he placed his hope.

Nugzar had much experience in the art of war, and he knew Xevi well. He didn't flatter himself that victory would be easy. He was ruthless and brave. Shedding blood was for him a form of entertainment, an enjoyable way to pass the time. However, he knew that Gocha and his army were a force to be reckoned with, and that the enemy was revered throughout the entire region.

One morning, at the break of dawn, a bearded man covered in steel armor entered the crowd of Mtiuletians. His gold-plated sword and his gilded helmet indicated that he was not an average Mtiuletian and probably belonged to a well-known and respected family. The outlines of his fat, smug face and his lips, so thick they turned in on themselves, his oversized nose, wide nostrils, and the swollen bags under his miniscule eyes all testified to his ruthless nature. His eyebrows joined together to form a single dark line above his eyes, which rendered them even more repellent. Furrows curled around his eyelids and spread over his face like the sun's rays on a parched desert. He was not a patient man.

He was standing in front of the crowd of Mtiuletians. They trembled as though united by a single feeling, took off their hats, bent their heads low, and said in unison: "Victory to Nugzar! Nugzar the Great! Nugzar our Leader!"

Nugzar nodded in mild displeasure and contempt, as though he wished to say that the Mtiuletians, so fanatically devoted to him, were barely worth his attention. He walked over to the spot, encircled by a fire, where a *nabadi* was spread out on the ground and kneeled. The Mtiuletians' soldiers stood nearby, watching their leader.

"Sit down. I have something to say to you," Nugzar said in a coarse voice.

The Mtiuletians kneeled on the grassy valley, in imitation of Nugzar, and waited patiently to hear what their lord, who had grown rich thanks to their help, would have to say.

"Mtiuletians! The Khandosxevians, the Chartlians, and the Gudamaqrians have all refused to help us." Nugzar thundered. "I swear by Mary, Mother of God, they'll pay for their refusal. I'll make sure every day of their lives will be bitter and the sun will never shine on them again. So much blood will flow from their veins that it will stain all their flowers red. I'll dress their widows in black and their corpses will be enough to feed all the vultures in the world. With my own hands I'll rip the hearts out of the bodies of anyone who tries to instigate them against us. I'll squeeze every last drop of blood out of their hearts with pleasure and I'll only be satisfied when I feel their last palpitation."

Nugzar stopped speaking for a few seconds as his eyes filled with an evil flame. Among the men who stood listening to him were mountaineers who had faced death a thousand times with a smile on their faces. The heat of the battle had tempered their hearts into steel, but, as they listened to Nugzar, even these brave men could no longer hold themselves back. Nugzar's words caused a shudder to run through their bodies. Everyone stood motionless and silent.

"But we'll leave that for the future," Nugzar continued. "We'll defeat the Moxeves. I didn't want a long, drawn-out battle. I hoped to annihilate them all quickly, but that's all right. Now, everyone will have to wave their sword twice as hard, but we will win in the end. There's no time to delay. Let's go!"

Nugzar had expected that his words would be met with cheers of approval. When he finished speaking, however, silence filled the air. Time passed, but the silence refused to dissipate. As Nugzar watched the Mtiuletians in shock, a flame of rage ignited on his face.

Unable to suppress his anger any longer, Nugzar yelled, "What the hell is going on?"

His words were once again met with complete silence.

"Is this treachery or are you all just pathetic cowards? How can you refuse to help me? Who is the traitor who refuses to stand by my side?" Nugzar began to scan the crowd in search of the culprit, with a threatening glare on his face, as though he intended to kill him with his eyes.

One Mtiuletian emerged from the crowd, made his way toward Nugzar, and stood directly in front of him.

"I am the one, sir," he said. "I am the one who refuses to follow you."

Nugzar reached for his sword and jumped forward to stab the young man in the heart, but restrained himself in time and replaced the sword in its scabbard.

"So you're the traitor? But, of course you're a coward. Who would ever take you for a man? You belong with the women. Go home and sit down by the fireplace among the women. You have no place on the field of battle. I'll easily find someone to replace you as commander of the troops and without a doubt he'll be braver than you."

The Mtiuletian waited patiently for Nugzar to finish speaking. He stood tall and motionless; only the slight trembling of his voice indicated that Nugzar's insults bore deep into his heart.

"Dear Nugzar, the king entrusted you with our welfare. The king's reputation is in your hands; his name stands as a shield to all of Mtiuleti. A Mtiuletian will never violate the orders of the king of Georgia. So why do you insult me? None of us agree to fight against the king. Not one of us will support you if you deceive him.

Nothing divides us from the Moxeves other than your infernal politics." The speaker then turned to the crowd and addressed them. "Isn't that right, my fellow Mtiuletians?"

"You're right. By the Icon of Lomisi, you're right!" A chorus of agreement ran through the crowd like a thunderbolt.

Nugzar observed the Mtiuletian in rage and disgust. He had never expected that things would turn out this way for him, but he was an experienced man, and knew that the smartest thing to do now was to suppress his anger. He calmed himself down and asked the crowd: "Just tell me one thing: Why did you promise to fight on my side?"

"You told us that we would attack the Ossetians, after we finished destroying the Moxeves. You lied to us! You told us that the Ossetians had risen up in rebellion against the king, and that the Moxeves supported them. That's the only reason we agreed to follow you."

"That's the truth. The Moxeves support the Ossetians, and we'll make them pay for their treachery."

"You lie! You lie!" the people yelled in unison.

Nugzar bit his lips in fury. He resolved to find out who had informed the Mtiuletians.

"Who told you I lie?" he thundered, hoping to discover the informer among the crowd.

"They told us themselves!" several men yelled in one voice.

"And you believed them?" Nugzar laughed. "What fools you are!"

"Why shouldn't we believe them?"

"They're afraid of you. That's why they said they weren't going to fight on the side of the Ossetians. They wanted to protect themselves from us."

"That's a lie!" the crowd yelled in response.

Nugzar turned blue from rage. He was not used to being treated with such disrespect. As he listened to the Mtiuletians' words, he felt the urge to squeeze everyone to pieces, to crush them all, turn them to dust and to scatter their remains over the earth. But he knew it was better to conceal his rage and he held his tongue.

"So you believed what they said?" Nugzar asked again.

"Yes, we believed them. By the Icon of Lomisi, we believed them!" several men repeated. "We believed them because the Moxeves came to us and swore that they didn't rise up against the king or support the Ossetians. They took an oath and struck the tree with their axes. No one who makes this oath ever goes back on his word. Isn't that right, Mtiuletians?"

"That's right!" everyone screamed. "The Moxeves won't deceive us. Let's go home." The crowd dispersed and the Mtiuletians headed back in the direction from which they had come.

The sound of their movements resounded for a long time, until they were concealed behind the mountains. Silence fell over the field. Only one man remained, standing alone on the empty field. Thoughts raced wildly through Nugzar's brain. His face was blanched white. He stood as still as a stone, powerless to move his body. Then, suddenly, he swung his head upward like a lion in rage, ground his teeth together, and growled:

"May you trample me with your feet, if I don't make you pay for today's treachery!"

XVIII.

At the entrance to the Trusso Gorge, where the narrow Tergi River frees itself from the rocks and stretches all the way to the field, stands the last Ossetian village on the Georgian border. It is called Okroqana. A large group of people had gathered here to pass the time in celebration. Though they were rejoicing, and it was clear from their incessant singing that they had good reason to be happy, it was equally clear that they had not assembled simply for fun. Not a single woman could be found among the group. The men stood armed from head to foot. Numerous horses were posted nearby, loaded down with goods. The horses struck the earth impatiently with their hooves and moved their legs back and forth.

The excited men moved about restlessly. It was clear that they had no intention of setting up camp for the night at the place where they were stationed and would soon be back on the road again.

They were in the process of delivering a toast when a dust cloud swept through the Trusso Gorge. The Ossetians suddenly stopped celebrating and stared at the dust cloud as it danced wildly in the wind and hurled toward the mass of people.

Several riders galloped forward, their outlines buried under layers of dust. Unable to see their faces, the Ossetians observed the dust cloud silently. Finally, the dust dissipated and the riders suddenly appeared mounted on their horses on a mountain peak not far away. The path facing them was so narrow that the horses had to jump from rock to rock as they made they way forward. The cliffs protruded as sharp as noses on the canvas of the sky. Ruptured suddenly from the earth, they sat mounted so proudly that the Ossetians found them-selves unable to tear their eyes away. The riders disap-peared behind the mountains, however, just as quickly as they had appeared, as though the earth had buried them forever.

"Nugzar! Nugzar is coming!" the Ossetians yelled joyously.

Yes, the man on horseback was indeed Nugzar Eristavi, galloping toward his faithful Ossetians, where they had promised to wait for him. They had gathered there in the expectation of uniting with the Mtiuletians and marching together onto the field of battle.

The Ossetians longed to annihilate the Moxeves, who stood like a wedge between them and the Kists, prevent-ing them from plundering other people and grabbing their territory. They wanted to trample the Moxeves, who, though surrounded on every side by foreign tribes, blocked the passage that led into the heart of Georgia.

They wanted to help Nugzar because after destroying the Moxeves, it would be easier to plunder and desecrate the other regions of Georgia. The Ossetians rejoiced as soon as they saw Nugzar, though they expected that he would arrive with the Mtiuletians following close behind, and were surprised to see him riding toward them accompanied by so few people. They had no idea that the Mtiuletians had returned home, because the Mtiuletians had traveled back home via a path that went through Lomisi Mountain rather than passing by the village of Okroqana, so that the Ossetians didn't have a chance to see them.

"But why is he coming alone?" The Ossetians whispered among themselves. "It's strange, by God!" They soon calmed down, however, when one of the Ossetians said to the others, "Probably the army is following behind and these men are just on a reconnaissance mission."

With these words, several men who had been chosen by the others to lead them in battle stepped away from the crowd, mounted their horses, and galloped toward Nugzar, eager to greet him.

The riders sang, shot their guns, and screamed in joy as they approached Nugzar Eristavi, who was descending the mountain path along with his companions. Nugzar's horse was exhausted, drowning in sweat, and breathing heavily. The Ossetians and Nugzar raced toward each other. They just barely managed to pull on the reins for their horses to stop when their foreheads nearly collided with one another. The horses stumbled backward onto their hind legs, their mouths gaping open, then stood as motionless as though their bodies had been carved of stone.

"*Pandag rast!*" Nugzar greeted them in Ossetian.

"*Da quta rast!*" the Ossetians yelled in response.

"How are things?" Nugzar asked. "Is everything going well?"

"We're doing well, thanks to God and to your help."

"Are you gathering the troops?"

"Yes. Everyone is here," answered one of the Ossetians who had been chosen to lead the others.

"Is anyone missing?" Nugzar asked cautiously. He did his best to appear calm, though his brows were furrowed in consternation and a bitter, mysterious frown was stamped on his face.

"After looking at you, who could say no to fighting on your side, oh Master?" the Ossetian replied obsequiously and then added, "Everyone is here, my Lord. Everyone is here and waiting to serve you."

Sparks of pleasure raced through Nugzar's heart. His face was suddenly illuminated, but the color soon faded and the gloomy expression he had worn earlier returned.

"I am grateful, grateful indeed, my Navruz!"

"How can you be grateful to me? I am unworthy to serve you. You are everything in the world to us!" Then Navruz turned to the crowd of Ossetians. "Isn't that right, men?"

"That's right! Nugzar is our master!" the Ossetians said in unison.

Nugzar remained silent. His mind was tormented by another problem. He was facing a difficult situation. The Ossetians were only brave and eager to fight because they thought that they had the support of the Mtiuletians. He knew well that if they found out that the Mtiuletians had abandoned them, it would be hard to keep them on his side. But what could he do to keep his influence over the Ossetians in place? What would happen when, inevitably, they found out the truth? Should he tell them everything at once or wait for time to tell?

Such were Nugzar's bitter thoughts. The question of how to solve this problem consumed his entire being, and the normally proud, talkative man, discovered to his consternation that at this moment, he could not pronounce a single word.

"I almost forgot, your honor!" Navruz exclaimed.

"Forgot what?" Nugzar asked.

"The man we sent to meet with the Lezgins has returned."

"He's returned?" Nugzar cried out, his eyes on fire. "Where is he? Show me right away!"

"He's over there, in the camp with the other men."

"And what news did he bring? Tell me! Tell me right away! Quick!"

"The Lezgins are on their way to help us. They'll be arriving this evening."

"Is that really the truth?" Nugzar cried out, but he soon managed to restrain himself, sat up straight on his horse, and, gritting his teeth, growled, "Now I know what to do."

After he pronounced these words, Nugzar's face suddenly changed. Whereas prior to this conversation, he had spoken in a soft and modest tone of voice, now his voice was as imperious as thunder.

"Let's go meet him. Tomorrow the sun will set on the life of every Moxevian." When he finished speaking, Nugzar stiffened his shoulders and cracked his whip against his horse's flesh until she strode forward at a

153

faster pace. A second later, he reached the camp on the outskirts of Okroqana and began issuing orders.

XIX.

Nugzar's movements were not concealed from the Moxeves. Every day, Moxeve soldiers penetrated into the Ossetians' rear guard and spied on them from all angles. Every day, they reported everything they learned of the enemy's progress back to Gocha. For their part, the loose-tongued Ossetians couldn't keep their secrets to themselves. Many times they sold all their inside information in exchange for a shirt's worth of wool.

One evening, when the sun had not yet completely set, Gocha called his people together. Once he said grace and gave his thanks to God, he cried out:

"People of Xevi! The Mtiuletians have refused to support Nugzar, but we still haven't been able to evade war. Instead of the Mtiuletians, now Nugzar is bringing the Lezgins against us. Why hide the truth? War is bitter and full of suffering. It forces mothers to dress in black and deprives parents of the touch of their children. Nugzar is a powerful and insatiable enemy when it comes to shedding blood. War is no joking matter, but the harder it is, the higher the stakes, the more precious the victory. What can we do, when an army ten times larger than ours comes to attack us? Do not fear, victory will still be ours, because God is on our side. They'll rush into our homes, destroy our villages, and rape our women. To die fighting such evil is bliss. Who will have the honor to die in such a manner? Whose heart beats steadfastly, whose shoulders stand straight? One for all and all for one!"

"May the man who runs away from the enemy marry his mother! May he who is afraid of death be damned by the Holy Trinity!"

"Amen!" The answer thundered through the crowd like a deep bass voice, as the mountains echoed back until the sound dissipated. The crowd stirred. Full of nostalgia for his youth, Gocha's eyes filled with tears. He could no longer restrain himself, and cried out:

"How I wish I was one of you young men, healthy and strong, rushing onto the field of battle. I wish I was one of you noble young men destined to die in defense of his motherland. I wish I was one of you whose path to heaven is already paved by your heroism."

After Gocha finished speaking, the crowd formed into groups around the wall which surrounded the church, where the meat of slaughtered animals was boiling in large pots. The animals had just been sacrificed to God in anticipation of the farewell dinner. After eating, the Moxeves said goodbye to each other, and went to their posts, from where they were to keep a look out for the approach of the enemy. Who knew on whose corpse the sun would rise tomorrow? Who knew whose eyes would be closed forever, or whose mother would shed inconsolable tears?

XX.

Dusk arrived, quietly extinguishing the light of day. The last rays of light sadly whispered farewell to the rays of the sun. The mist fearlessly arose from the earth and dissipated like smoke over the green field. In the village of Sion, an order was issued from the church's bell tower for the guards to take their places. The sound of the bell twinkled like the memory of grief in the damp, saturated air. The guards appeared particularly restless; everyone's brows wore the stamp of concern. Their faces had turned into ears and eyes; the slightest movement could not be concealed from them. In case their eyes couldn't see, their ears were perked to detect any movement. They were in the position of a man who waits with great agitation for something to occur. The Moxeves had been informed that by tomorrow night Nugzar would attack them. Everyone was busy preparing for this battle. They had no time to lose and threw their caution to the wind.

During this period of general preparation, someone opened the door to Gocha's bedroom and stopped on the threshold. The old man had thrown his hat off, knelt down in front of an icon of the crucifixion, and was praying intensely. He raised his head and directed his eyes toward heaven. His heart beat fast, and the blood rushed through his veins. His hair, always so carefully arranged, was now in disarray, and his veins protruded from under his wrinkled skin. He didn't speak, but it was clear from his facial expression that an ominous feeling weighed heavy on him, and his heart was pressed on all sides by a river of blood.

The intruder watched Gocha from the threshold, afraid to violate the sacred silence. He too was overcome by emotion. First he stood petrified. Then he bent his head and fell to his knees. Suddenly, in the middle of the old man's prayer, the spectator heard the old man pronounce his name. "Dear God, make my child Onise worthy of your grace." Onise gasped upon hearing these words, and the old man gasped when he realized that someone was observing him. He arose with effort and dragged his legs toward his son. Then he placed his hands on Onise's head and intoned in a voice full of trepidation:

"God, keep my child pure. Kill him before he shames himself."

As he said these words, the old man's cheeks overflowed with tears. He quickly wiped them away and looked around, afraid that someone had seen him crying. Onise could no longer repress the feelings that stirred inside him. The sight of his father crying made Onise soften as well, and his eyes sparkled like the sun in the midst of rain. He felt how much his father loved him; he imagined to himself what his father must feel to see his child facing the danger which awaited the young men of Xevi. Soon, the sword would glisten in the rays of the moon which illuminated the field and its shrill whistle would mix with a groan from far away. Who can say whose face would stiffen into a smile? Who knows whose feelings would suddenly be cut short and whose body would freeze like a glacier?

"Father, why are you crying?"

"Who knows what will happen to you?" Gocha whispered.

"Who says anything will happen to me?" Onise tried to console his father. "By the mercy of God, we'll turn back the enemy and return home in peace."

"The will of God always prevails," the old man said, his hands trembling. "Go, Onise. Now is the time. May God protect you! If you die, that too is the will of God. We're born once and we die once! I just ask you to die like a man. Die in such a way that Xevi won't be ashamed to bury you."

"You'll see, Father. I'll fulfill all your expectations."

"Don't forget where your ancestors were born and buried, where their bones are interred. The enemies want to take that land from us, but don't let them have it. Your ancestors also shed their blood to defend this land, and like them, we must suffer to defend it. Thanks to their courage, a river of blood flows all the way from here to the underworld. Now you, the brave men of Xevi, have the chance to show what you can do."

The old man paused, stared at his child, and several times made an effort to say something more, but the words stuck in his throat. Finally, he waved his hand and pronounced weakly: "Good. Now go."

Onise left quickly and headed for the place where he was to stand as guard. Gocha stared motionlessly at his son from the threshold of his home, until his silhouette was covered forever by the walls of the house. Then he groaned, rubbed his furrowed brows, and said: "Now it's time to go see to the army."

XXI.

When Onise left his father, he headed for Narovani, where the mountain path ended and where he was supposed to keep watch for the approach of the enemy. He walked along the path with his customary care, when he saw someone move a rock in front of him. Onise jumped to the other side of the road, hid himself behind a large stone, and waited for the approach of the stranger who had violated the sacred silence of the night.

A good deal of time passed before anyone appeared on the twisty road. Finally, footsteps echoed in the air, softly at first, but gradually growing louder, as a woman approached with a man walking alongside her and their donkey trailing behind, loaded down with food. It was clear from their clothes that the man and the woman were shepherds, bringing cheese down from the mountains to the army in the field.

Onise was certain that the couple approaching him were Moxeves. He stepped away from his hiding place, then heard his named pronounced, hurried back behind the stone, and froze, tense with anticipation.

The couple spoke loudly; it sounded as though they were arguing. They came even with Onise and sat down on a large stone.

"Woman," the man began, "by God, I told you that I can't endure this anymore. You've crushed me. I've spent my soul waiting for you and I can't wait anymore.

"What do you want me to do? I told you that I don't love you."

"So this is what happens after all I endured! The flame that burns inside my heart is enough to make a desert out of all the oceans in the world. Maybe death is the only way out! Then we would both be at peace."

"When will you leave me alone? What do you want from me? Do you think you can make me love you by force?"

"You expect me to leave you alone? You're my wife. I have my manhood to think about."

"So what do you want me to do?"

"I want you to remember that you are my wife."

"Why don't you just give up? I told you I don't love you, and that's the last thing I have to say to you on this subject."

The man sat silently for several minutes with his head hung low. Lightning suddenly filled his eyes.

"Don't say that, woman! You should at least have pity on yourself, even if you have no mercy for me."

The woman raised her eyebrows in surprise. "I have no pity for myself! If you kill me, I'll be at peace!"

"So it will never be? You'll never love me? You'll never be mine?"

"No."

The man reached for his sword, but suddenly stopped.

"So you want to be his? You think I'll allow this? What makes you think I'll ever hand you over to him? I'll kill you both and then myself before I'll allow anyone else to experience the joy you refused me."

"Then kill me! Just don't hurt anyone on my account. Why do you want to punish others for my deeds?"

The woman sidled away from her interlocutor, and began to glare at him. The man jumped to his feet in rage.

"So you want to die? All right, I'll kill you, but not until I cut off Onise's head and bring it here for you to see."

With these words, he rushed onto the road and ran off in the direction of the camp where Onise intended to sleep that night. The woman screamed, ran to the slope behind which Gugua disappeared and shouted after him: "Gugua! Gugua! Don't destroy me! Why are you doing this? This is worse than death!"

She ran to the edge of a cliff nearby, which over-looked a vast, empty expanse, and was preparing to jump, when she felt a warm hand grab her and pull her back, away from the cliff's edge. The woman fell back-ward into the arms of her protector and struggled to pronounce the one word which she had the strength to utter: "Onise," she whispered. "Onise."

XXII.

They passed a large part of the night together. The moon illuminated the clear, fresh air and spread its gentle rays over the land. Onise and Dzidzia sat motionlessly in a single place, enslaved by the fire of love that burned in-side them. Neither of them was fully conscious of what they were doing. Overcome by the sweetness of being together, they drank the nectar that only lovers can taste. The rays of the moon gently played on Dzidzia's pale face, which tormented Onise with its sweetness as he embraced her furiously and kissed her like a madman. Every touch, every caress that passed between them resembled the soft wind blowing above them and swaying the willow branches gently. They forgot where and who they were. They only cared about one thing as their bodies and their souls merged into one.

They were wrapped inside this oblivion when all of a sudden a gunshot pierced the air and sent the lovers to their feet. Onise, who had up until this moment paid no attention to the prodding of his conscience, now remembered that it was his responsibility to protect the Moxeves from a surprise attack by Nugzar Eristavi's troops. The bitter reality of what had just happened squeezed his heart. Before his eyes rose the picture of Gocha praying fervently for his only son. He recalled with a pang what his father had said before he left for the last time, when he didn't know if he would ever see his son alive again. Onise's imagination was assaulted by a horrifying picture of his dead friends, slaughtered because they had trusted him and let themselves fall asleep, while he had carelessly neglected to keep a lookout for the approach of the enemy.

The rapid gunfire grew louder. Shots flashed like lightning and the fire proliferated like a thousand tongues, consuming the lives of young men, eager to die in defense of their homeland.

Onise stared at Dzidzia in rage; his head swarmed with accusations: *You witch! You enchanted me here to destroy me!* he thought to himself. *Farewell, manhood. Goodbye, dignity.*

He determined to compensate for his carelessness and save his friends by sacrificing his life, and he ran down the mountain to join the battle, but he soon realized that it was too late even for that. The enemy had penetrated Moxeve territory; they already had crossed the first trench, which the Moxeves had dug to delay the approach of the enemy. Onise saw the enemy's flag swaying in the air, hoisted over his friends' corpses lying in a heap near the entrance to the village.

XXIII.

Onise raced to the scene of the massacre with his eyes fixed on the ground and his mind in torment. He knew what he had to do. The enemy had taken the Moxeves' first trench and killed practically all the brave men who had given themselves for their homeland. Onise only understood how much his moments of bliss had cost him once he stood gazing on the pile of corpses. The best men of Xevi had perished because of him, those young heroes who didn't even have the chance to show their courage in battle. Onise's conscience began to torture him. A mysterious emotion somewhat like grief filled his mind and tore his heart to pieces.

He looked like a madman. His hat had fallen off his head, his clothes were in disarray and his hair was disheveled. His eyes swirled wildly inside their sockets. He could no longer make sense of anything. Every word, every thought, changed as he tried to fasten onto it as to an anchor, a refuge in a sea of confusion. He ran toward the enemy's regiment. Only one thought filled his mind: to die by the same sword that had slaughtered the corpses of his innocent friends.

Onise had almost reached the field, where the victorious Ossetians were trampling on the corpses of the faithful, honest Moxeves, shouting "Hoorah!" and preparing to return to their camp, when he collided with the few Moxeves who had survived the attack on the trench he was supposed to have guarded.

"Who are you?" the Moxeves asked the crazy man racing toward them, as they barred his way and placed the barrels of their guns against his heart.

"It's me!" Onise screamed, his voice equally full of rage and grief. "Kill me! Kill me! I'll be grateful to you forever!"

"My God, Onise!" one of the Moxeves cried out and everyone laid down their weapons.

"Thank God you're alive!" a second Moxeve said.

Onise gazed at his friends, his heart full of sorrow, his eyes sparkling. He determined that those Moxeves who had remained alive should know about his cowardly act. Now they were making fun of him. He burned with an invisible fire, all the more powerful in that it ignited every corner of his body and filled his soul.

"Kill me! That's what I deserve. Kill me, by God! Don't have mercy on me!" Onise begged his companions as tears flooded from his eyes. "Kill me, I tell you! I'll be grateful to you! Are you blind? Aren't you shocked to see a man crying in front of you like a woman?"

The Moxeves watched Onise in astonishment, unable to figure out why he was behaving so strangely.

"So you're not going to have mercy on me? You want to torture me? You're deceiving yourselves, by God! It's not going to be like that! Onise will never show himself again. He won't let the enemy mock him. Are you happy?" Onise laughed bitterly and ran off in the direction of the enemy's camp.

After they recovered from their astonishment, the Moxeves realized Onise's intentions, ran after him and caught him.

"Where are you going? What are you doing, you poor boy? Have you gone out of your mind? What's wrong with you?" they yelled at Onise, as he struggled against them and tried to free himself from their grip.

"What do you want from me? Why do you hold me like this? I want to die in the place where my friends perished. If you don't let me then I'll kill myself!" Onise announced, as he lifted the body of the gun and placed it in his mouth. Someone snatched the gun from his hand.

The Moxeves, thinking that he had gone crazy at the sight of all his dead friends, realized that there was no hope of bringing him back to his senses, disarmed him, tied his limbs together, and carried him away.

"You beasts! What do you want from me?" Onise begged his friends to let him go, tears pouring from his eyes. "Why don't you just let me die? What good is my shame to you?"

He continued raving, though his strength gradually abandoned him and he became silent. No one paid attention to his ravings anymore; the Moxeves were still in a dangerous situation and had to hurry to catch up with Gocha and their fellow soldiers.

XXIV.

They walked forward as a group, as quiet as the dead.
Everyone's face had a somber expression; their lips were
closed shut, and their eyes were aflame. Their situation
was all the more difficult because they hadn't had the
chance to fight the enemy. They felt like they should
either have surrendered, run away like women, or
stretched out their necks like lambs on the slaughtering
block for Nugzar's bloodthirsty army to slash with their
swords.

The young men who dreamed of dying in battle had
been assaulted so suddenly that they had not even managed to fire a single shot. Who knows how many young
lives were spoiled in that uneven attack, how many boys
who were the pride of their community and the hope of
their neighbors breathed their last during those fateful
moments, leaving behind only the songs that would be
sung in their honor every year, when someone remembered who had died that day and why.

What awaited those who remained alive? In the
mountains, a person who spoils a battle through his
recklessness becomes the laughingstock of his village.
On the other hand, defeat in battle is always a great misfortune. Everyone hates recklessness, and humiliation is
the lot of careless fools, while the defeated are met with
pity and compassion.

The Moxeves were so full of despair that they
couldn't make sense of what had happened, how Nugzar's army had managed to steal upon them so suddenly,
without them hearing or suspecting anything.

Only one thing consoled them: they had managed to take captive three men whom they had caught on their side and whom they suspected of working as spies for the enemy's army. More likely than not, it was these men who had brought Nugzar's army into Xevi and surrounded the Moxeves before they even knew they were being attacked.

Among those they had taken captive there were two Ossetians who had run away from their own people and found shelter in Xevi. The Moxeves always knew that these Ossetians might betray them at any moment; their treachery was no surprise, but the third captive's identity baffled them and made their hearts sink. He was a Moxeve himself, and his presence alongside the other captives cast a pall of shame over all of Xevi.

Onise followed the group, worn out, weakened, his soul spent, his life barren of meaning, unable to fix his eyes on anyone or anything.

"Onise, have you been captured, too?" Onise suddenly heard someone ask him. He turned and stared in astonishment at the speaker.

Before his eyes stood Gugua, his face blanched white, his body trembling all over.

"Gugua!" Onise managed at last to shout, and pointed to the rope which bound him. "What happened to you? Why are you tied up?"

"They accuse me of treachery." Gugua said vaguely and spit on the ground in suppressed rage.

The two friends had endured much together, and Onise knew full well that Gugua would never betray his people. Besides, even if Onise had not decided to give his friend the benefit of the doubt, he remembered well that he had seen Gugua together with Dzidzia. He had heard their conversation with his own ears, and he knew perfectly well that Gugua had raced to the army's camp with an entirely different goal in mind than one of betrayal. He had intended to kill Onise; Onise had become his enemy, and the cheated husband's heart yearned for revenge.

"Maybe," Onise wondered to himself, "Gugua knew that everyone was relying on me and his desire to have his revenge on me turned him into a traitor?" Onise furrowed his brows and ground his teeth. Gugua stared at him, as though awaiting an answer. "Why don't you say anything?" Gugua began.

"What is there to say?"

"So you don't have anything to say?" Gugua said bitterly, and added, "Fine. I'll be quiet, too. Thank God everyone thinks I'm guilty. Otherwise, your days would be counted. This is your day. The sun shines for you. Let it shine. That's God's will. I have no fear of death, but woe to him who betrays his brother."

After he finished speaking, Gugua bent his head in pain; a fiery brand seemed to burn his neck. He sighed and moved away from Onise, squeezing the last drop of hope from his former friend's heart.

XXV.

The day had not yet parted from the night when the army of Xevi came to life. They discovered that Nugzar's army had taken their first trench and that only a few Moxeves were left alive inside. Thirsty for revenge, the Moxeves demanded:

"Blood! Blood! Blood for the deaths of our brothers!" the people screamed in one voice. There was only one man standing in the crowd who hadn't lost control of himself. No matter what the situation was, he always found time to think rationally and to examine the problem from all angles.

This man was Xevisberi Gocha, who summoned those few Moxeve soldiers who remained alive to gather around him in the trench. Gocha had placed all his faith in his son, who has been assigned to stand watch over the trench. How was it possible, Gocha wondered to himself, that this tragedy had happened while his son was supposed to be keeping a lookout for the approach of the enemy?

"Tell me," Gocha began as soon as he reached the place where his soldiers stood. "Tell me quickly. How did this happen?"

"What's there to say?" one of the Moxeves answered. "Two Ossetians—Becherai and Tapsiruqo—went to the enemy and showed them the best route to attack us."

The Moxeve stopped speaking. Gocha waited impatiently for him to continue. His heart trembled with an unpleasant foretaste of disaster.

"So you didn't catch anyone else?" Gocha asked and furrowed his brows.

"If only your words were true!"

"Who else did you catch? Tell me his name!" Gocha demanded, his eyes on fire. He stared at his interlocutor so intently that the power of his glare forced the Moxeve to utter the name of the third traitor."

"Who else was there?" Gocha repeated.

"Gugua."

"What? What did you say?" the old man asked in shock. He thought that perhaps his ears had deceived him. He wanted to say more, but the words stuck in his throat.

"Gugua," the Moxeve repeated.

It pained Gocha to hear his neighbor called a traitor, and the pain was even sharper because that neighbor belonged to his flock. Gocha felt responsible for Gugua's moral direction and implicated in everything he did.

The old man directed his eyes toward the sky. "Lord, in what way have we offended you, that you have allowed brother to betray brother?"

Gocha's heart burned with shame for all the people of Xevi. He feared that Gugua's treachery would serve as a bad example and have a negative influence on the community. He stood motionless, absorbed by the thoughts which creased his careworn face. At last, he wiped his hand across his forehead. Several times, he looked at the Moxeve who had uttered Gugua's name as though to ascertain whether what he said could really be true. His eyes implored and reproached his interlocutor at the same time.

What made the old man, the leader of Xevi, implore and reproach Gugua, a simple soldier, with such desperation? Gocha had one child, Onise, who was one of the Moxeves supposed to guard the first trench. Now, however, Onise was nowhere to be seen. Where was he? Gocha wanted to know. Where had he been? Why didn't the Moxeve who uttered Gugua's name say anything about what had happened to Onise? If he had died, then why didn't he tell Gocha about his son's heroic death and try to comfort his sorrow-filled heart?

Gocha tried to imagine everything that could have possibly happened to explain Onise's absence and negligence. His patience was soon exhausted. He gathered the last of his strength to ask a final, fateful question:

"Where is Onise? Why haven't you told me what happened to him?"

"Onise! The poor boy! He's out of his mind. If we hadn't been there to save him, he would have the enemy destroy him, by God."

Gocha calmed down slightly after receiving this answer; at least his child was alive and had acted in a manner worthy of his ancestors. What more could he ask for?

"Where is he now?"

"He's calmed down a little bit, and now he's with his companions," the Moxeve answered. "He's a pitiful sight to see." I wonder if he'll ever return to sanity."

The old man was satisfied with this answer and felt as peaceful as he could be expected to feel, given the situation. "Tell the other men to tie up the captives," he ordered, "and to watch over them carefully. We'll call upon God and ask him to wreck vengeance on our enemies."

After Gocha finished speaking, he headed for the spot where the troops had already gathered and were hurriedly preparing to launch a new attack against the enemy.

XXVI.

When Gocha arrived, the soldiers divided into three regiments. With their leaders at the head, they set off in the direction of the enemy. They had resolved to capture the stronghold that Nugzar had seized from them earlier and to attack his troops from three sides. This was the only way to pay back the enemy for the destruction he had caused. Everyone felt that the outcome of this battle would determine the fate of Xevi for many years to come.

The young Moxeves raced toward the enemy with a smile on their face. They knew that the task they had consecrated their lives to was a holy one. If they met with death, they knew that their name would be remembered by their community, that it would pass from mountain to mountain, that their sacrifice would not be forgotten. If, in this world they could look forward to the bliss of glory and fame, then, after death, a heavenly award awaited them. They believed that they were defending with their lives their people, their faith, their identity, their native land. For them, rushing to death was a form of celebration. Their yearning to collide with the enemy on the field of battle was all the more intense after the memories of their slaughtered brothers stirred their hearts and made their souls cry for blood.

Onise was among those Moxeves who rushed to attack Nugzar's army. His normally joyous face was marked by sorrow. His lips were sealed and the skin stretched taut as though he were an old man. His eyes bulged from their sockets, as though they wanted to explode from their joints, and the veins on his cheekbones pulsated with blood. Onise was generally brave and self-sacrificing by nature, but today he was twice as reckless as he usually was because the mistake he had made weighed heavy on him. He hoped to compensate for his sins by sacrificing himself.

Several men had been entrusted to Onise. Together they formed the front ranks of the Moxeve army. His men believed in him; they trusted that he would do everything in his power to protect them. Their plan was to approach the enemy without being noticed, and then either capture or destroy them before there was time to figure out what had transpired. This was supposed to happen quickly, so that the enemy wouldn't be able to figure out what was going on and would not have time to mount a defense. Onise tried to carry out the plans exactly as he had been instructed. He ran in front, his eyes and ears leading him. The other soldiers followed in their leader's footsteps so carefully that their own steps left practically no trace.

They were afraid of disturbing the silence by a slight movement of their feet which would thereby attract the attention of the enemy. Sharp rocks punctured the surface of the ground, so they approached stealthily with sandals covering their feet. With every step forward, they used their toes to test the firmness of the soil. Suddenly Onise flung himself to the ground. The others imitated him then took out their swords and waited motionlessly.

Several minutes of silence passed before five men suddenly appeared on the horizon from the enemy's side. Onise lay still as they rushed toward him. When all five of the enemies reached the spot where they were laying, he jumped to his feet. The other Moxeves followed their leader's example and a few seconds later the Ossetians who had been sent ahead on a reconnaissance mission fell to the earth as their bodies began to twitch. The more the blood flowed from their wounds, the more desperately they struggled for life.

It all happened so fast that the Ossetians didn't have time to scream. The Moxeves, after finishing their work, set forth on their road and reached their destination as the dawn rose on the enemy's camp. There they hid themselves and waited in ambush. The enemy's camp was completely silent. They passed the time peacefully, emboldened by their recent victory and certain that their guards were watching out for them. Nugzar was convinced that the Moxeves would be too afraid to fight back and expected that they would soon send their representatives to him to negotiate a surrender. He could never have imagined that such an outnumbered people as the Moxeves would dare challenge his power, particularly now that he had a large army of well-trained and heavily armed Lezgins on his side.

Without being noticed, the Moxeves attacked Nugzar's army from three sides, and surrounded him. Suddenly, the roar of gunfire shook the air. The Lezgins jumped to attention, but they were so confused by the approach of the Moxeves that they didn't know what to do. They ran from one corner of the camp to the other, unable to decide from where to begin shooting. The Moxeves didn't give them time to come to their senses; they ran toward them and annihilated everyone in sight. Amid the general chaos, a single warrior stood out, mounted proudly on his white horse, watching the destruction below. This was Nugzar, who held a sword in his right hand and swung it in all directions, killing anyone he could reach. Several Lezgins sat mounted on their horses alongside their leader. The fire of heroism burned in their hearts, unlike the Ossetians, who preferred to escape danger rather than confront it.

Onise raced into this battle, drunk on his courage, killing anyone who crossed his path. In search of a fierce battle he ran to where the most blood was being shed. It seemed that his body was protected by a magic spell, because no matter how many men he fought, no matter how powerful they were, he emerged unscathed. The Moxeves watched him in awe. Their hearts filled with pride as he attacked without sparing his own life.

Suddenly, Gocha appeared on the top of a slope that overlooked the enemy's camp. His white hair lay in disarray on his head; the strong wind tangled it even further. The tip of the flag that he held in his hand unfurled in the wind and his gold cross glistened proudly. Gocha's horse stepped forward arrogantly, as though she too was conscious that her master had been selected by the people of Xevi to be their leader and that they placed all their faith in him. The old man pulled on his horse's reins and galloped toward the place where Nugzar and several of his men were still battling the Moxeves.

"Moxeves!" Gocha addressed them. "All you brave young men, follow me!" A crowd of Moxeves quickly gathered round him and surrounded Nugzar and his few remaining men.

A windstorm swept through the plain. Dust covered everyone. The sun's rays grew dim. The vigorous fighting which until then had covered the battle field was replaced by the grinding of teeth and moans. Weapons rattled in the air, obscuring the sound of grief.

From time to time, Gocha's flag rose from the heavy waves of dust that saturated the air and tempered the Moxeves' hearts into steel. Suddenly, the people sprang to action and began to shout.

The wind scattered dust everywhere over the plain. The corpses of Nugzar's soldiers were piled into a high heap that rose like a tower over the Moxeves. Gocha stood nearby, his sad eyes directed toward the sky, a blank expression on his face. In the distance, a group of people running away from the scene of the slaughter could be made out; this was Nugzar, mounted on his horse, followed by the few remaining men in his army who had miraculously managed to avoid annihilation.

XXVII.

The people had buried their dead, but they still hadn't dispersed, and instead remained by Gocha's side. They were certain that Nugzar would not attempt to attack them again any time in the near future.

In one spot of the mountain, the leaders of the army and the *temi* sat together on rocks arranged in a circle. The deacons were also present, holding the flags of the villages. In the center of the circle stood Xevisberi Gocha. The circle was open on one side only, nearby which the rest of the community had gathered. Nervous excitement could be discerned on everyone's faces. Someone gazing at them from afar would not have been able to determine whether they were grieving over lost loved ones or awaiting another tragedy. Gocha and the other members of the *temi* bent their heads and silently pondered the events of the past day. The crowd watched and waited in fear for the *temi* to speak.

Finally, Gocha lifted his head and gazed at the crowd, his eyes filled with grief. Onise stood in front of the crowd and watched Gocha closely. His body trembled and he bent his head because he could no longer stare into his father's face. Gocha looked at his son, but he rapidly removed his eyes and said in a quiet, but firm voice:

"Bring in the criminals."

The crowd divided down the middle. The two Ossetians and Gugua soon stood in front of the jury selected by the *temi*. The people watched them, waiting impatiently for the Almighty to decide their fate.

"Untie them," Gocha ordered. His order was rapidly carried out.

Gocha rested his elbow on his knee, and placed his head on the palm of his hand. He waited impatiently to hear what the criminals had to say. The eldest member of the *temi* stood up, walked to the center of the circle, bent down on his knees, and said,

"People of Xevi, listen carefully! Before you stand two Ossetians. Six years ago, they entered our community. They swore to us that they had been exiled by their community and could never return, because they had killed a man by accident and would be punished with death if they returned home. We pitied them and took them into our homes. We all know that death is never a good thing. It's a sin to kill, but, when a person is desperate, he can kill himself as well as others. Every death, even if it's an accident, is a tragedy. We saw the Ossetians as victims of this tragedy. They asked us for a portion of bread and shelter. It is not in keeping with Xevi traditions to hide from their guests. We don't say no to people who ask us for help. We gave the Ossetians a place to sleep, and we built them a home and provided them with land. We made them our brothers and offered them a peaceful life. And how did they repay us for our generosity? They showed our enemies the road to our camp and led them to victory. They put the enemy on the tracks of those who had given them a bed on which to lay their heads, a hearth on which to warm their food, and a roof to protect them from the rain. They decided to betray us. What do we say to this, people of Xevi? I have told you everything, for you ought to know every detail if you are to pass a just verdict. A man's death is not a matter to be taken lightly."

Xevisberi Gocha rose from his knees, bowed in all directions, and took his seat.

"Justify yourself if you can," Gocha ordered them, still seated. Agitation swept through the masses of people gathered below.

The Ossetians fell to their knees and begged for mercy but the jury was deaf to their pleas. The jury grouped in a circle around Gocha and discussed the problem for a few minutes. Then they took their seats again. Gocha lifted his head and said in a voice that resembled thunder:

"Stone them both!"

The people cheered when they heard his words, and the color drained from the Ossetians' faces. One of them approached Gocha, who bent his head again as soon as he finished speaking and became immersed in thought.

"Gocha, have mercy on me!" The Ossetian cried out. "I'll be your slave! I'll do anything for you! Just don't kill me!"

"Stone them!" Gocha repeated in the same imperative voice.

"But why do you want to kill me? Why must you stone me?" The Ossetian screamed and jumped to his feet. "You can kill me, but I won't let you live either."

With these words, the Ossetian pulled out from under his *choxa* a sword he had been hiding all this time. The crowd rushed on the Ossetians and crushed them to death. When they dispersed, both corpses lay limp on the ground. Gocha watched the proceeding without moving from his place, his head as always resting on his arms. The only expression visible on his face was hatred, which burned in his eyes as he stared at the slaughtered Ossetians.

XXVIII.

When the Ossetians' bodies had been carried away, Gocha said calmly,

"Bring in Gugua."

Several men approached Gugua, untied his hands and brought him forward. Gugua staggered, his eyes unable to concentrate on the scene in front of him. Soon, however, he managed to regain control over his movements and stood still.

Gugua's face had turned entirely white. His mouth parched, he stood in front of the people, fixing his blank gaze on a spot in the crowd.

The crowd spat curses at him and pointed their fingers in his direction. As with the Ossetians, one of the leaders of the *temi* emerged from the crowd and delivered the official accusation.

He accused Gugua of being at the lead of the group of Nugzar's army who attacked the Moxeves. Without a doubt, the accuser said, Gugua too had shown the enemy the best way into the Moxeves' camp.

"Justify yourself, if you can," Gocha said, and then fell silent.

Gocha groaned bitterly and surveyed the crowd until he caught sight of Onise, who stared back at him, petrified. Gugua's eyes sparkled. His face turned red with the fire that burned inside. He staggered forward in Onise's direction, and then restrained himself again. Then he turned his face, distorted by grief, toward the jury, and, as though his hat was burning his head, ripped it off and flung it to the ground.

"Say whatever you have to say in your defense!" Gocha repeated. Only the slightest undertone in his voice indicated how miserable he was.

"What should I say? What can I tell you?" Gugua said bitterly. "God knows that I didn't commit the crime you charge me with, but I was seen with the enemy and who will believe me now? Why do you torture me with these questions? Why do you try to make me speak? Kill me and then you'll be at peace!"

"Boy, it's easy to die," Gocha said after several minutes of silence. Fervent love was audible in his voice. "In my heart I don't believe it possible that a man of Xevi, raised on this soil, and nurtured on her breast, would ever betray his brother, sell his friends, and bring down destruction on his native land. No Moxeve who discovers that his brother is capable of treachery, can live in peace. His heart will always be full of grief and there will be no end to his sorrow."

Gugua took hope from these words. He saw that Gocha regarded him with the love a parent feels for his child. At that moment Gugua would have given anything to convince the old man that he was innocent. "Gocha, by God, in the name of the guardian angel of Xevi, I swear by my youth, I swear by your reputation, I am not guilty of the crime you accuse me of. However, I cannot prove my innocence. Therefore, I must be punished. I must be killed."

"What were you doing in the enemy's camp?"

"What was I doing? You want me to tell you everything? Leave me alone, Gocha. Don't force me to speak. You see how difficult it is for me to talk. By all the goodness in your heart, why are you torturing me?"

"Gugua, the Lord knows I will never be at peace until I find out the truth. Every word, every question, penetrates my heart like a sword, but the laws of the *temi* matter more than our suffering. So tell us everything."

"Everything? All right!" Gugua yelled and fixed his eyes on the spot where Onise was standing. Gugua's pathetic face became distorted again, as though he was weighed down with a great weight. Life no longer showed on his yellowed face. Gugua lifted his head high and turned to the jury.

"Listen to me. I have no fear of death. Even if I justify myself, I'll never be allowed to live. Now that I have nothing left to live for, why should I lie? Listen to me. I'll tell everyone the truth. I was coming down from the mountain and when I reached the plain, I ran into the enemy. I tried to run away to inform my brothers waiting in the trench about the enemy's approach, but the soldiers from the enemy camp followed me and I couldn't escape in time. They didn't shoot me because they were afraid of attracting attention to themselves by the sound of gunfire. I tried to shoot them, but my gun was broken and the trigger wouldn't fire. Then my brothers saw me with the enemy and took me for a traitor. If I am lying, may this earth split beneath my feet and swallow me alive!"

"What were you doing on the mountain?" one of the *temi* members asked Gugua.

"I had business."

"Were you alone?"

Gugua didn't answer, and the jury member repeated his question. "Were you alone?"

It was clear from his trembling lips that a struggle was going on inside Gugua's mind. He didn't want to utter the name of the woman whom he still loved more than anyone else on earth.

"What does it matter, whether I was alone or not?" Gugua said at last. "You had to interrogate me like this to find out whether I betrayed you. I told you that I didn't betray you, that I didn't sell my brother. However, I know that these explanations won't save me from punishment! Don't ask me anything else. I won't answer you. At least let me have a few moments of peace before I die!"

Gugua fell into silence after he finished speaking. He crossed his hands over his chest and stood motionless, pretending to be mute to the questions that were directed at him.

The *temi* encircled Gocha for a long time, discussing what the punishment should be, while the people waited impatiently. Clearly, they were having a hard time reaching a decision. Gugua's silence and the agony of uncertainty weighed like a boulder on Onise's shoulders.

Suddenly, when the crowd's patience had nearly evaporated, the *temi* took their seats. Everyone sat down, and after a few minutes of silence, Gocha stood up.

"Dear God," he began. "We wish to heed your words. Forgive us if we have deviated from your wishes in any way. For Xevi to be at peace Gugua must be isolated and exiled forever. He must never be allowed to see his village or family again. He must be condemned to wander the earth forever! Only his wife has the right to follow him into exile. From this day forth, no one shall warm him if he sees him shivering, offer him water if he sees him suffering from thirst, or feed him if he sees him starving. Every home will be closed to him, everyone will be deaf to his pleas. By the gods and angels of Xevi, may your rage fall on anyone who betrays his people."

Suddenly, someone placed his hand on Gocha and stopped him from speaking. "Stop!" ordered a familiar voice.

The crowd stared in amazement at the man who dared to touch Gocha, particularly when he held the holy flag in his hand. Onise was standing before them.

"Stop, Xevisberi!" Onise repeated. His hair was in disarray and his eyes bulged from their sockets as though about to fall from his face. "Gugua is right!"

The crowd became excited and restless. Gocha lifted the flag high and thundered, "Silence!" An ominous silence fell over the crowd. Then Gocha turned to Onise. "Repeat what you said," he ordered his son.

"I said that Gugua was right," Onise said. "Don't punish him in vain. Gugua and I have a reason to be enemies. When he was coming down from the mountain, he was looking for me because he wanted to kill me. But then he collided with the enemy and now you're falsely accusing him of treachery."

"Who told you that I wanted to kill you?" Gugua asked, his eyes on fire from jealousy.

"I heard it with my own ears. When you were speaking, I was also on the road, hidden behind a tree. I can't lie anymore! I am drowning in my brothers' blood! Their death was my fault. I lost my mind. I couldn't see the enemy coming. It's my fault, but everyone is blaming Gugua." Onise raced to finish, to utter everything on his heart, because his body was trembling and he didn't know how much longer he could continue speaking. His words struck the astonished crowd like thunderbolts.

The old man stared at his son in shock. He seemed to have temporarily lost the power of speech, and it took him some time before he came back to his senses. At last, he moaned, wiped his hand across his face, frowned, turned to his son and said:

"So that's how you understood all that I've taught you? Cursed be your name! May you be hated everywhere and by everyone. The ghosts of your ancestors have risen from the dead! They cry out for vengeance! May you get the punishment you deserve!" After he finished speaking, the old man turned to the jury, "Your brother's blood calls upon God to reveal his power! Now it's up to you to determine the punishment for this traitor to his people!"

The jury members whispered to each other in distress. Finally, the leader of the *temi* approached Gocha and said quietly, "Gocha! Your son did not betray Xevi. His youth got the better of him and made him act carelessly."

"That's even more reason why we should punish him. It's not for nothing that a man has a beard and a conscience. Onise is already dead to me. May he be burned alive!"

185

"Gocha!" the members of the jury tried to calm him down, but they couldn't do anything; rage spread across the Xevisberi's face.

"Onise must die!" Gocha thundered. "He deserves to die. If you're afraid to apply justice, then I'll kill him with my own two hands." He pulled out his sword and lunged at his son, screaming, "You traitor! You don't deserve to live!"

He stabbed Onise in the chest, and his son fell to the ground, trembling. Gocha's sword penetrated to the center of Onise's heart. The murder was executed so quickly that no one had time to realize what was going on, much less to stop the shedding of blood.

Overcome by panic, the crowd ran in different directions. No one dared approach the old man, whose eyes roamed wildly over the corpse of his child. Bulging veins distorted his face. Anyone would have taken him for a madman.

At last, someone placed his hand on Gocha's shoulder and uttered his name.

"What?" the old man asked vaguely and looked up to see Gugua standing in front of him.

"Gocha!" Gugua repeated, this time in a louder voice. "I told you that I wasn't to blame, but I can't live after such shame has fallen on my shoulders. A brave man doesn't go back on his words. Farewell, Gocha! Goodbye, my people! May peace be with you!" Then he took out his gun, placed its barrel in his mouth, and fired, spraying his brain into the air.

The old man only groaned, looked around him in fear and gasped. Finally, he stood up, began to tremble, and flung away the bloody sword which he had been holding in his hands all this time. He stood motionless and silent for some time. Then, overcome by dizziness, he fell to his knees, and embraced his child. After several more minutes of silence, he began to cry out Onise's name and wrapped his body around his son's corpse.

Gocha wept for a long time over Onise's frozen corpse. Finally, he lifted his head, looked around, and jumped to his feet in terror.

"Go away! Go away!" Gocha cried and reached out his hands, pushing the air away from him. "This blood! My sword! My child! What happened? My child! Where is he now?" Gocha screamed into the air and began roaring like a wild beast.

Eventually, calm fell over all of Xevi. Life assumed its usual course.

From that day hence, the people of Xevi avoided that spot in the forest which crazy Gocha had turned into his home. If anyone was foolish enough to pass by, crazy Gocha would nag him with questions about his child. Then he would invite the stranger inside and tell him about Onise. Gocha would wax eloquent about how he was eagerly awaiting his son's return from somewhere far away. Then he would begin to threaten the visitor and demand that he tell him what he had done to his son. Such visits generally ended with the unsuspecting stranger scared out of his wits.

So passed the old man's days, until the moment when, one particularly harsh winter, the snow buried him as he made his way through a narrow mountain passage and silenced him forever.

As for Dzidzia, no one has heard anything about her ever since that evening on the mountain when she kissed Onise for the last time.[11]

1884

---

[11] Every word of this story was told to me by Ghinja Xuleli, a very old Moxeve. [Qazbegi's note.]

Afterword: Aleksandre Qazbegi's Mountaineer Prosaics[12]

Once, when he was herding sheep in the mountains, the Georgian prose writer Aleksandre Qazbegi was approached by two travelers, a Frenchman and an Englishman.[13] The travelers wanted to know where they could buy wool to take back home to Europe, but did not know in what language to address the "savage" shepherd. The travelers gossiped together in French about the mountaineer barbarity, not suspecting that the mountaineer facing them was follow-

[12] An earlier version of this afterword appeared as "Aleksandre Qazbegi's Mountaineer Prosaics: The Anticolonial Vernacular on Georgian-Chechen Borderlands," *Ab Imperio: Studies of New Imperial History in the Post-Soviet Space* 15.1 (2014): 361–390. This version has since been revised.

[13] A slightly earlier text that uses an encounter with a Frenchman to comment on conceptions of civilization difference among Georgians, Russians, and Europeans is Ilya Chavchavadze's "Letters of a Traveller" (1871), discussed below. Whereas Chavchavadze's French interlocutor conveys the inferiority of Russian civilization vis-à-vis Europe, Qazbegi uses humor and irony to question even broader civilizational dichotomies.

ing every word of their exchange. Unbeknownst to them, this Georgian writer-turned-shepherd had been educated in French and read Maupassant in his leisure time. Eager to shock his auditors, Qazbegi announced in fluent French that there are many sheep in the mountains and wool is easy to find.

Not content with the shudder of surprise he induced in his interlocutors by his fluent French, Qazbegi decided to prolong his pleasure with yet another revelation. He replied to the travelers' praise of his French that most shepherds in the mountains spoke the language far better than he did. "Almost all our shepherds speak French," he told the Europeans. "I've been living in other places, far from these mountains, so my French is rusty, but, as for the other shepherds, you wouldn't be able to distinguish them from native French-speakers."[14] The European travelers were dumbfounded. "We thought you were barbarians!" they exclaimed in unison.

Already in this humorous self-representation, the Georgian prosaist used the figure of the mountaineer to parody a colonial discourse that based its claim to civilization on Europe's putative distance from non-European barbarians. As literary theorist Gary Saul Morson reminds us, parody acquires a specific life in

---

[14] Aleksandre Qazbegi, "Namtsqemsaris mogonebani (1883)," in *Txzulebata sruli krebuli otxri tomad* (Tbilisi: Sabchota Sakartvelo, 1948–), 1: 445. Future references to Qazbegi's works are to this edition. For a reading of this work that emphasizes its engagement with ethnography, see Emzar Kvitaishvili, "Kartuli dokument'uri prozis mshveneba," *Literaturuli ziebani* 21 (2001).

prose. Parody's evolution within Georgian literary culture is thus intimately related to the life of prosaic forms within the vernacular anticolonial imagination.[15]

The stories in this collection show how, when Georgia was incorporated into the Russian empire, ethics became ethnologized as a virtue specific to the mountaineers. The primary targets of this romantic ethnologization were Muslim Chechens, protagonists of stories like "Eliso" and "Elberd" (also by Qazbegi; not translated here). Against the political landscape that divided the north from the south Caucasus, and thus separated Georgians from their Chechen brethren, Qazbegi perceived the mountains as a landscape inflected by ethical values that, because they belonged to the domain of everyday life, were best expressed in prose. Qazbegi's contemporary, Urbneli (N. Xizanishvili), voiced similar values in his ethnographic writings. Urbneli contrasted his approach to that of the Russian Romantics, especially Lermontov and Pushkin, who were drawn to the Caucasus by virtue of its "loveliness" and for whom the "sublime landscape" was "pure art" rather than "the truth and reality of life," to his own vernacular ethnography. Using "aesthetic" negatively to suggest a way of seeing that commodifies the object of perception and impedes contact with the world, Urbneli complains that "Europe views Georgia primarily from an aesthetic perspective, and this is why the contents of our life remain uninves-

---

[15] Gary Saul Morson, *The Boundaries of Genre: Dostoevsky's* Diary of a Writer *and the Traditions of Literary Utopia* (Evanston: Northwestern University Press, 1988 [1981]), 107–115.

tigated [and] unknown to others."[16] (His statement, incidentally, rings true in the present.) As a prosaist and crafter of an anticolonial vernacular, which here signifies not a new language *per se*, but rather a new aesthetic orientation, Qazbegi followed Urbneli's injunction: he gave literary form to mountaineer life by conjoining ethnography with prose.

Like the protagonists in these stories, Qazbegi was a mountaineer, albeit one who had received a Moscow education at the Agricultural Academy, and prior to that at a classical gymnasium. As noted in the preface, he was born in 1843 in Stepancminda (St. Stephan), a village high in the mountains of Xevi, into a family that belonged to the Georgian nobility (*azanauri*).[17] Situated near Ingush and Chechen territory, Xevi was incorporated into another, imperial, geography by the colonizing process that was initiated in these mountainous regions during the early decades of the nineteenth century.[18] After he returned from Moscow in 1870, unable to com-

---

[16] N. Xizanashvili (N. Urbneli), "Mgzavris shenishvnebidgan [From the notes of a traveler]," *Droeba* 129 (1883), 2.

[17] For a collection of primary source documents concerning Qazbegi's biography, see Vano Shaduri, *Masalebi Aleksandre Qazbegis biograpiisatvis: Qazbegebis sagvareulos moghvatseni* (Tbilisi: Tbilisis universitetis gamomcemloba, 1985). For a valuable Soviet ethnography of Xevi, see Sergi Makalatia, *Xevi* (Tbilisi: Saxelmtsipo gamomcemloba, 1934).

[18] For the Russian colonization of the Georgian mountain regions, see Austin Jersild, *Orientalism and Empire: North Caucasus Mountain Peoples and the Georgian Frontier, 1845–1917* (Montreal: McGill-Queen's University Press, 2002).

plete his education due to a financial crisis brought about by his father's death, the young Qazbegi shocked his family with the news that he had decided to become a shepherd for the next seven years of his life. This was the occupation in which Qazbegi was engaged when he crossed paths with the French travelers.

Qazbegi spent much of these years, 1872–1879, wandering the mountains and sleeping under the stars, exposing himself to the mountaineers' sufferings and struggles, and becoming persuaded that their lives were connected to an ethical system that was beyond the ken of the Georgians residing in the plains. Qazbegi's literary career began when he ceased to be a shepherd and left the mountains for cosmopolitan Tbilisi in 1879, where he lived until his death fourteen years later. During these decades, Tbilisi was a city where the majority of the population was Armenian and Azeri. Unlike in the Georgian highlands and Imeretia (western Georgia), Georgians were in the minority.[19] Alongside his consis-

[19] For the population of Tbilisi (called at that time Tiflis) during the eighteenth and nineteenth centuries, see M. Polievktov and G. Natadze, *Staryi Tiflis v izvestiiakh sovremennikov* (Tiflis: Gosizdat Gruzii, 1929), 41–49. Among many works on the topic of Tbilisi cosmopolitanism, see Paul Manning and Zaza Shatirishvili, "The Exoticism and Eroticism of the City: The 'kinto' and his City," in *Urban Spaces after Socialism: Ethnographies of Public Places in Eurasian Cities*, eds. Tsypylma Darieva, Wolfgang Kaschuba and Melanie Krebs (Frankfurt/Main: Campus Verlag, 2011); and in the same volume, *idem*, "Why are the Dolls Laughing? Tbilisi between Intelligentsia Culture and Socialist Labour"; Paul Manning, "The Theory of the *Café Peripheral*: Laghidze's Waters and Peripheral Urban Modernity," *Forum for Anthropology* 7 (2012): 189–210.

tent focus on the lives of his fellow Moxeves (Georgian mountaineers from Xevi), Qazbegi's ample attention to Chechens' and Circassians' encounters with colonial rule afforded an unprecedentedly detailed perspective on the interface between Georgian and Muslim mountaineers' lives.

Georgian attitudes to their mountaineer neighbors have inevitably been inflected by the agendas of the empires that have passed through the Caucasus. From the middle of the nineteenth century, Russian policies profoundly shaped Georgian attitudes toward mountaineers. Georgia came under the influence of Russian imperial rule long before the tsarist army began to make substantial incursions into the northern Caucasus. When Alexander I annexed Georgia in 1801, he violated the Treaty of Georgievsk that the Georgian King Irakli had signed with Russia in 1783.[20] This treaty had nominally guaranteed Georgia's independence and promised continuation of the ancient Bagrationi dynasty in return for giving Russia permission to oversee Georgia's foreign affairs.[21] The resentment of the Georgian nobility toward the coercive imposition of Russian sovereignty, including Russia's violation of the terms of the Treaty of Georgievsk, led to uprisings against Russian rule, first in Kaxetia in

[20] For a Georgian account of these events, see Zurab Avalov, *Prisoedinenie Gruzii k Rossii* (St. Peterburg: Montvid, 1906). Also see David Marshall Lang, *The Last Years of the Georgian Monarchy: 1658–1832* (New York: Columbia University Press, 1957), 183–184.

[21] For the original text of the treaty, see G. G. Paichadze, *Georgievskii traktat* (Tbilisi: Mecniereba, 1983).

1812, and then, even more dramatically, to a foiled re-bellion in 1832.[22]

And yet, even as they rejected the coercive imposi-tion of Russian sovereignty, the Georgian nobility felt that their aristocratic lineage obliged them to serve in the imperial army. This experience, which was a rite of passage for many Georgian poets, meant that the literary elite disproportionately contributed to the conquest of the north Caucasus and its annexation by Russia during the second half of the nineteenth century. This they did with great success, attaining to the highest ranks and honors. Their experience on the battlefield did much to enrich Georgian literature.[23] Georgian aristocrats, par-ticularly the poet Grigol Orbeliani (1804–1883), helped to bring to an end the anticolonial Islamic state fash-ioned by Imam Shamil, united Chechnya and Daghestan into a single political entity, and withstood Russian in-cursions for an astonishing quarter-century (1834-1859).[24] The Georgian literary elite's complex position

[22] For the 1812 uprising, see Akaki Gelashvili, *Kaxetis 1812 tslis ajanqeba* (Tbilisi: Artanuji, 2003). For the 1832 attempt to bring Rus-sian sovereignty to an end, see Stephen Jones, "Russian Imperial Administration and the Georgian Nobility. The Georgian Conspir-acy of 1832," *Slavonic & East European Review* 65.1 (1987): 53–76.

[23] For an important study of the Georgian poetry generated by this experience of war, see Harsha Ram and Zaza Shatirishvili, "Romantic Topography and the Dilemma of Empire: The Caucasus in the Dialogue of Georgian and Russian Poetry," *Russian Review* 63.1 (2004): 1–25.

[24] For Orbeliani and Russian culture, see Igor Semenovich Bo-gomolov, *Grigol Orbeliani i russkaia kultura* (Tbilisi: Izd-vo Akademii nauk Gruzinskoi SSR, 1964). For Orbeliani's role in quelling an

between anticolonial resentment on the one hand and imperial desire on the other generated as many contradictions in the domain of literary form as it did in the domain of geopolitics. Qazbegi profited from the ambivalence that haunted the literary tradition within which he worked. By way of reacting against it, and seeking a more firmly oppositional stance to Russian rule, he elaborated a critique of industrial modernity, and of the barbarian/civilized dialectic on which it was founded.

These concluding pages explore Qazbegi's prosaics of the colonial encounter through three related lines of inquiry. First, I consider some European sources for Qazbegi's prose. Second, I consider Qazbegi's uses of local narratives pertaining to the Muslim Chechens residing on Georgia's mountainous borderlands, alongside the Moxeves. Thirdly and finally, I trace the place of a Georgian anticolonial vernacular prosaics within world literary history.

Fiction and Ethnography

Early modern Georgian poets of the sixteenth and seventeenth centuries made it possible to express poetic norms in the Georgian language, thereby creating a new linguistic reality from the interface between a local lan-

anticolonial uprising in Guria (western Georgia) in 1841, see Stephan Jones, *Socialism in Georgian Colors: The European Road to Social Democracy, 1883–1917* (Cambridge: Harvard University Press, 2005), 295n31.

guage (Georgian) and a global one (Persian).[25] Working in a historical moment marked by the interface of Georgian and Russian rather than Georgian and Persian, Qazbegi infused this literary language which had, for most of its history, been addressed primarily to a courtly elite and which had verse as its preferred medium, with a new vernacular, informed by the dialects spoken in the mountains. He broke with what Paul Manning has described as the Georgian manuscript culture that excluded non-aristocrats, who were "spoken of savagely in the way that one might speak of someone who cannot talk back."[26] Manning has carefully tracked the implications of this shift from manuscript to print culture from the perspectives of linguistic and historical anthropology.[27] My interest here is with what this transformation meant, over the longue durée, for the aesthetic status of Qazbegi's chosen medium. In transposing a literary language crafted in Tbilisi's urban spaces to the mountains, Qazbegi created a landscape and a medium for themes

[25] For early modern Georgian recreations of a Georgian vernacular on a Persian basis, see Rebecca Gould, "Sweetening the Heavy Georgian Tongue: An Early Modern Georgian Appropriation of Jāmī's *Yūsuf and Zulaikhā*," in *A Worldwide Literature: Jāmī (1414–1492) in the Dār al-Islām and Beyond*, eds. Thibaut d'Hubert and Alexandre Papas (Leiden: Brill, forthcoming). I do not of course intend to imply that Georgia had no literature prior to the early modern reinvention; rather I wish to indicate that the tension between Georgian and Persian during the early modern period anticipated the similarly productive tension between Georgian and Russian in a later period.

[26] Manning, *Strangers*, 116.

[27] See "Describing dialect" and *Strangers*, respectively.

that had, at the time of his writing, not yet been incorporated into the Georgian literary repertoire.

Qazbegi's prose rendered Georgian highlanders' ways of speaking and imagining into a literary idiom. These were the people concerning whom the Georgian critic Chreladze described in Georgia's most prominent nineteenth-century newspaper, *Iveria,* as "generally pathetic, poor shepherding people, wrapped in ragged old skins with the fur turned inside out."[28] "Whenever we encounter them," Chreladze continued with disdain, "we must grin, for on seeing them we can't stop ourselves from laughing. We considered both the man and the women of the mountains to be equally ridiculous." Even though he was writing after Qazbegi's major works had been published, Chreladze's evocation of the elite's contempt for the mountaineers pertained to an age before dialectical difference had become central to Georgian prosaics.

While he appreciated the new aesthetic Qazbegi introduced to Georgian literature, Chreladze was still inclined to despise the vernacular dimensions of mountaineer culture, which were reflected in acute form in the mountaineers' speech. The mountaineers whom Chreladze saw as "children of misery" constituted for him an

---

[28] St. Chreladze, "Chveni mtis xalxi: sabibliograpio tserili [Our Mountain People: A Bibliographic Letter]," *Iveria* (1892), 1. Cited and discussed in Manning, *Strangers in a Strange Land: Occidentalist Publics and Orientalist Geographies in Nineteenth-Century Georgian Imaginaries* (Boston: Academic Studies Press, 2012), 306n18. I am grateful to Paul Manning for providing the full citation beyond the material cited in his book.

undifferentiated homogenous mass. "All dress the same way and have the same life," Chreladze marveled. "Even their names don't resemble names! The mountaineer husband to be calls his fiancée 'woman' (*kalau*) while [his wife-to-be] calls him 'man' (*vazhau*)." The very heterogeneity of mountaineer life was thus an object of ridicule as late as the 1890s, and in Georgia's most influential periodical. Qazbegi's anticolonial vernacular had to wait until after the author's death to attain its rightful place in the Georgian public sphere.

When Georgian poets turned away from Persian culture and began looking to the north, their models were Pushkin and Lermontov. Georgian poets such as David Guramishvili (1705–1792) and Nikoloz Baratashvili (1817–1844) crafted new idioms from within their encounters with modern European, particularly Russian, poetry.[29] The new Romantic generation was increasingly hostile to the Persian literary influences that were seen to betoken Georgia's backwardness. Now, instead of criticizing the Persian Shahs and Ottoman Sultans, whose power was in decline and therefore posed no challenge to Russian, let alone Georgian, sovereignty, Georgian poets of the colonial era preferred the European rhetoric of the sublime to the unsublime culture of Caucasus mountaineers. Guramshvili and Barastahvili do not encompass the entirety of Georgian literature,

[29] For Baratashvili's poetics, see the recent collection edited by Gaga Shurgaia, Luigi Magarotto, and Hans-Christian Günther, *Nik'oloz Baratashvili: ein georgischer Dichter der Romantik* (Würzburg: Königshausen & Neumann, 2006).

and some Georgian poets idealized the mountaineers just as Georgian Romantics idealized Russian and European civilization. But for the most part, the anticolonial vernacular imagination orientation pertains to a later moment in Georgian literary history.

Poetry, Fiction, Ethnography

Qazbegi's counterpart in the domain of poetry, Vazha-Pshavela (1861–1915), heralded the anticolonial vernacular turn with his poems dedicated to the mountaineers of Pshavi and Xevsuretia.[30] Just as Qazbegi's fictions were ethnographically informed by explanatory footnotes and the use of local languages (see for example "Eliso"), Vazha's poetry was enriched by his ethnographies, which documented the life ways of the mountaineers whose tribulations he rendered in verse.[31] Given the convergence in their aims, which coexisted with a divergence in their chosen mediums, it should come as

---

[30] Vazha-Pshavela is one of the most widely studied Georgian poets and the scholarly corpus on his work is dense. Key works in European scholarship include Kevin Tuite "The banner of Xaxmat'is-Jvari: Vazha-Pshavela's Xevsureti," in *Der Dichter Vaza-Psavela: fünf Essays*, ed. Ekaterine Gamqrelizde (Würzburg: Königshausen & Neumann, 2008), 11–37, and Luigi Magarotto, "La poésie epica di Važa-Pšavela," in *Georgica I*, ed. Luigi Margarotto and Gianroberto Scarcia (Rome: Arti grafiche Scalia, 1985), 7–48.

[31] Vazha-Pshavela, *Etnograpia, polklori, kritika, publicistika, korespondenciebi* (Tbilisi: Sakartvelos SSR saxelmtsipo gamomcemloba, 1956).

Fig. 9. Qazbegi (left) and Vazha-Pshavela (right).

no surprise to see Georgia's two major vernacular writers with their arms on each other's shoulders, in a
memorable picture taken at the height of their respective
careers (figure 9). Vazha's example, like Qazbegi's, illus-

201

trates that being a vernacular intellectual entailed more than making choices about dialects and languages, although such decision-making figured into the vernacular intellectual's vocation. More importantly, a vernacular intellectual was someone who, contrary to the preferences of many of his peers, grounded his aesthetic vision in precolonial and local culture. During the same era in the north Caucasus, the Chechen Umalat Laudaev and the Daghestani Bashir Dalgat epitomized this process. When they undertook to render mountaineer life in prose, they did so in ethnographic rather than strictly literary genres.[32]

This close interface between fiction and ethnography across multiple Caucasus literatures suggests that Kevin Tuite's argument that "it is in the domain of literature that the ethnographic concept receives particularly original elaboration," made with respect to Georgian material, tells us much concerning the specificities of Caucasus literary history.[33] This sequence through which Georgian literature's vernacular turn was inaugurated, first in ethnography and only later in fiction, substantiates Manning's claim that "factual descriptions of life,

[32] For Laudaev, see footnote 45 below. Dalgat authored many major studies of mountaineer belief systems, including *Pervobytnaia religiia chechentsev i ingushei* (Moscow: Nauka, 2004) and *Rodovoi byt i obychnoe pravo chechentsev i ingushei: issledovanie i materialy 1892–1894 gg.* (Moscow: RAN, 2008).

[33] Kevin Tuite, "Ethnographie et fiction en Géorgie," in *Célébrer une vie: actes du colloque en honneur de Jean-Claude Muller*, eds. Kiven Strohm and Guy Lanoue (Montréal: Département d'anthropologie, Université de Montréal, 2007), 170.

including genres like ethnography, are in fact the primary genres of 'realism,' and literary forms [are] strictly secondary and parasitic."[34] Like Tuite, Manning advances his argument with reference to a Georgian archive, but this sequence (ethnography first, followed by its aesthetic recreation in fiction) broadly elucidates the process through which the vernacular turn was instantiated, and the anticolonial vernacular was formed and refined, across the Caucasus.[35]

Beyond being the first modern Georgian to write intelligibly and sympathetically about Muslim mountaineers, Qazbegi was both inheritor and critic of the geopolitical and interconfessional burdens of Georgian history. A lone figure in his lifetime, Qazbegi's mediation of Georgian and Russian literary and geopolitical relations parallel the ways in which the sixteenth- and seventeenth-century Persianizing Georgian poets Teimuraz I and Nodar Tsitishvili engaged with the Persian literature of Safavid Georgia. This parallel however falters when one considers the place of ethnography in Qazbegi's aesthetic, and how it marks a new horizon, and a new space for the vernacular, in Georgian literary culture. Another major difference between Qazbegi and his Persianizing predecessors who worked within an elite literary culture accustomed to textual circulation through

[34] Manning, *Strangers,* 306n17.

[35] For South Asianists such as Subramanian Shankar (*Flesh and Fish Blood: Postcolonialism, Translation, and the Vernacular* [Berkeley: University of California Press, 2012]), vernacular realism is "a realism *aspiring* to reproduce the local in all its specificity," but for contexts that are not exclusively local (11).

manuscripts is that his fictions promote prose as a medium for aesthetic form and print as the medium for its dissemination.

In an important study of the interface between fiction and ethnography in Georgian literary history, Tuite distinguishes between anti-ethnography, a method that, he argues, situates its characters in distant geographies to comment allegorically on Georgian cultural traits, and pseudo-ethnography. The latter is distinguished from anti-ethnography by its physical location within Georgian territory, and by its deployment of a fictional ethnographer "who speaks with an author's voice."[36] Anti-ethnography is ethnography's inverse: it deploys ethnographic methods in distant, and often fantastical, contexts. Pseudo-ethnography by contrast uses ethnographic methods in culturally proximate, and hence seemingly realistic, contexts, but with non-Georgian characters, whose foreignness defamiliarizes a familiar geography. In terms of Tuite's typology, Qazbegi's mountaineer fictions are pseudo-ethnographic endeavors to incorporate the allegorical force of anti-ethnography, which facilitates Qazbegi's political critique. Tuite supplements his typology with the important insight that anti-ethnographies (Rustaveli's medieval epic *Knight in the Panther's Skin* is his quintessential example) transpire in non-Georgian geographies because the distance from familiar Georgian landscapes brings psychological extremities into greater relief than mimetic representation.[37] While Tuite associates anti-

---

[36] Tuite, "Ethnographie et fiction en Géorgie," 165.
[37] Tuite, "Ethnographie et fiction en Géorgie," 164.

ethnography with medieval Georgian literature and pseudo-ethnography with Georgian literary modernity, Qazbegi conjoins the two typologies into a single, coherent aesthetic.

Vernacular Nationalisms

Qazbegi entered Georgian literature in an era when poets such as Baratashvili had begun, under the influence of Romanticist trends from continental Europe and Russia, to replace Georgia's historically eastward orientation with a new outlook directed toward Europe. While Qazbegi was influenced by the Romantic poets who preceded him, the authors who inspired him most, including Maupassant and Dostoevsky, were prosaists. Like Dostoevsky in particular, Qazbegi was deeply affected by the increasing relevance of journalism to the public sphere. Whereas the "first independent, privately owned daily in Russia" appeared in 1863 under the title *Golos* (Voice), under the editorship of A. A. Kraevskii. Within three years of that date, Georgia developed an indigenous tradition of print culture, represented most prominently by *Droeba* (Times), edited by Ilya Chavchavadze (1837–1907) until he broke away from the editorial collective to found *Iveria*.[38] By providing a home for

[38] The phrase with reference to *Golos*, is from Katia Dianina, "The Feuilleton: An Everyday Guide to Public Culture in the Age of the Great Reforms," *The Slavic and East European Journal* 47.2 (2003): 188. For *Droeba*, in addition to Manning, *Strangers*, see Elguja

occasional writing, the serial newspaper created a space for a genre that could blend "the personality of the author, with his individual literary background and ideological perspective."[39]

For genres like the *feuilleton*, a short sketch that became one of the most popular "serial [*gazetnykh*] genres, accessible and legible to the widest circle of readers," the newspaper's eclectic blend of narrative genres had the effect of making "this inherently journalistic form of writing almost border on fiction."[40] In contrast to modern newspapers, the majority of these Georgian serials were "composed more or less entirely of occasional correspondence" and in particular the *feuilleton*, which was categorized within this rubric of correspondence. Comparing the concept of the public sphere pioneered by Benedict Anderson through his study of print culture's homogeneous simultaneity with its Georgian counterpart, Manning identifies the main difference in the fact that "the public, Georgians, that is readers of *Droeba*, were also by and large imagined as potential *writers* to *Droeba*—correspondents.[41] The interface between reader and writer was more intimate in Georgian print culture

Chaduneli, *Gazet "Droebis" publicistta sazogadoebriv-ekonomikuri shexedulebebi* (Tbilisi: Mecniereba, 1969); and L. Berzenishvili, *XIX saukunis kartuli demokratiuli presa: glexobis sakitxi gazet "Droebis" mixedvit, 1866–1885 tsts.* (Tbilisi: Mecniereba, 1981)

[39] Dianina, "The Feuilleton," 194.

[40] For these citations respectively, see A. V. Zapadov, *Russkii feleton* (Moscow: Gos. izd-vo politicheskoi lit-ry, 1958); and Dianina, "The Feuilleton," 194.

[41] Manning, *Strangers*, 163.

than in Southeast Asia and other territorially extensive imperial domains that have shaped the Andersonian conception of nation formation through print culture.

More than other theorists of literary form, the Russian literary theorist Bakhtin appreciated how prosaists such as Dostoevsky, and the genres in which they worked in their journalistic writings, like the *feuilleton,* contested the poetic norms of preceding generations with a realism that extended "the limits of human sympathy, to make literature appear to be describing. . . reality itself."[42] Bakhtin clarified prosaics' ethical implications when he asserted that it was impossible to incarnate an individual "into the flesh of existing sociohistorical categories." "There always remains," Bakhtin insisted, "an unrealized surplus of humanity [*izbytok chelovechnosti*]."[43] This surplus of humanity is the origin of empathetic consciousness in Qazbegi's anticolonial vernacular prosaics. By rendering the mountaineers' vernacular life ways, including their ways of speaking, thinking, and their everyday tribulations, Qazbegi's prosaics speak to the Bakhtinian ethics of novelistic discourse, albeit with a political edge unforeseen by the Russian literary theorist.

The transformation in literary norms described by Bakhtin has long been understood in terms of the

[42] George Levine, *The Realistic Imagination: English Fiction from Frankenstein to Lady Chatterley* (Chicago: University of Chicago Press, 1981), 8.

[43] Mikhail Bakhtin, "Epos i roman" [Epic and the novel], in *Voprosy literatury i estetiki. Issledovaniia raznykh let*, ed. S. Leibovich (Moscow: Khudozhestvennaia literatura, 1975), 480.

changing sociology of literature and of literary form. The less understood vernacular reorientation entailed in this shift is brought into acute relief in the case of Georgian, a literature that was newly engaging with the non-elite stratum of society, including mountaineers. Compared to Russian, Georgian writers prior to Qazbegi were more interested in creating alliances with past literary traditions than in cultivating mountaineer aesthetics. Early modern Georgian poets invariably looked to Safavid Persia for their literary norms. By contrast, the second half of the nineteenth century witnessed a new kind of vernacularization that actively cultivated dialectical registers within the literary language, but which, most significantly for the purposes of this argument, was demographic, social, and political.

Across the Caucasus, poets and prose writers came to regard indigenous cultures as sources and stimuli for creative work rather than as mere backdrops for evocations of past times and places. In Armenia, Khachatur Abovyan (1809–1848) composed his novel *The Wounds of Armenia* (1841) before disappearing from the world. In Chechnya and Ingushetia, the ethnographers Laudaev, Dalgat, and the Ingush Chakh Akhriev introduced ethnography to the northern Caucasus.[44] The confluence of

---

[44] Laudaev's monograph on the Chechens was published under the title "Chechenskoe plemia" [The Chechen tribe], in *Sbornik svedenii o kavkazskikh gortsakh* [Compendium of research on the Caucasus mountaineers; henceforth *SSKG*] 6 (1872): 1–62. For an introduction to Akhriev and his writings, see L. P. Semenov, *Chakh Akhriev* (Vladikavkaz: Ingushskiii nauchno-issledovatel'skiii institut kraevedeniia, 1928).

the vernacular turn and ethnographic writing in the Caucasus calls to mind Bakhtin's postulate that the interaction between literary prose (*khudozhestvennaia proza*) and living rhetorical genres (*zhivye ritoricheskie zhanra*), which are "journalistic, moral, and philosophical," characterizes literary—one might add here *vernacular*—modernity.[45] This congruence of genres is also attested in the suggestion of an anonymous contributor to *Droeba* that a 'literature of the people," might be "salvaged," in its raw form and refined into a "work of poetry" by literate members of educated society (*sazogadoeba*).[46]

During the same years that in Russia, Nikolai Leskov (1831–1895) was busy making rural Russia legible to the metropolitan readers in St. Petersburg and Moscow, in Georgia, Ilya Chavchavadze was occupied with making the mountains landscapes—and, less comprehensively, the mountaineers themselves—a source for his prose. While Chavchavadze's "Letters of a Traveller" (1871) posits "a close, almost organic connection between the voice of nature, in the form of the Terek River, and the voice of the people," Qazbegi's anticolonial prosaics foregrounds human agency in settings that threaten to crush it.[47] In Manning's framing of this literary genealogy, "Chavchavadze's thematic focus on the mountain-

---

[45] Mikhail Bakhtin, "Slovo v romane" [Discourse in the novel], in *Voprosy literatury i estetiki*, 82.

[46] A.K., "Mcerloba," *Droeba*, No. 32 (28 March 1876), 1.

[47] Cited in Manning, "Describing dialect," 29. Terek is the Russian name for the river known as Tergi in Georgian.

eers of Georgia as a privileged locality for [the] pristine Georgianess of speech and custom" resulted in "the immense explosion of realist ethnographic and folkloric literature dealing with these regions . . . beginning with the ethnographic and literary writings of the Moxevian writer Aleksandre Qazbegi."[48] The shift from Chavchavadze to Qazbegi exemplifies multiple dimensions to Georgian literature's vernacularization: a movement away from a prose genre, the travelogue, that drew its ideology from the culture of the colonizer and that moved within the poetics of the imperial sublime, was followed by Qazbegi's anticolonial fictions that derived their themes, and to some extent forms, from indigenous ethnography. While Chavchavadze and Qazbegi were both influenced by Russian precedents, Qazbegi supplements Chavchavadze with a sustained critique of Georgian elite literary culture, waged through the chronotopic rhetoric of prose.

Over the course of the long nineteenth century, Armenian, Georgian, Vainakh (Chechen-Ingush), and Daghestani vernaculars attained new heights of clarity and sophistication. Each of these vernacular orientations made the people newly central to the construction of autochthonous national identities, and as new foci of authorial interest. Concurrently, authors from the Cau-

[48] Manning, *Strangers*, 57. Another work relevant to the subject of Qazbegi's debt to Georgian folk culture, Jemal Jaqeli's *Kartvel mtielta polkloruli traditsiebi Al. Qazbegi shemokmedebeshi* (Batumi: Gamomcemloba "Sabchota Ajara," 1974), is at present inaccessible to me.

casus evinced a new interest in ethnographic forms and conventions, through which they forged a vernacular aesthetic to suit a new affective register.[49] Their renewed interest in narrative was also reflected in the popularization, as well as the serialization, of the novel and the short story, both of which entailed new strategies of representation. Qazbegi is the most eminent representative of these vernacularizing trends in Georgian literature during the nineteenth century, in part because he cultivated an anticolonial vernacular that was sociological, political, and aesthetic in equal measures.

Anticolonial Prosaics

Even since Qazbegi transformed Georgian fiction, Georgia's mountaineers have been treated in Georgian literature as the bearers of sanctified traditions lost to Georgian lowlanders. Qazbegi's novel *The Parricide* (*Mamis mkvleli*), published in 1882, carries this idealization further than had been seen before in its narration of the star-crossed lovers Nunu and Iago. Nunu and Iago's dream of marriage is threatened by the ambitious and cruel tsarist officer Girgola. When Girgola kidnaps Nunu, the Chechen Parcho and the Georgian Koba save the innocent Nunu from the officer's malicious intentions. Through such conventional plots, Qazbegi's

---

[49] For the interface between ethnography and journalism in the Georgian context, see M. Xintabadze, *Kartuli polklori da gazeti "Droeba"* (Tbilisi: n.p., 2005).

mountaineer protagonists demonstrate the values that Georgians relinquished when they joined the Russian conquest and waged war against their mountaineer neighbors.

During and after the Russian conquest, Georgian intellectuals asserted—and occasionally fabricated—European affiliations for themselves and their literature. Given Russia's outstanding poetic tradition, such affiliations were most easily consolidated in verse. Assimilation to Russian cultural norms meant acquiring civilization's external trappings, but, even though the pace of Georgian literary production did not cease, the aesthetic of the imperial sublime could not accommodate the anticolonial vernacular.[50] As Qazbegi knew well, every cultural adaptation is political, and every language, in the words of Bakhtin, constitutes "a concrete opinion, insuring a maximum degree of mutual understanding in all spheres of ideological life."[51] Especially during the early Soviet period, Georgian poets such as Titsian Tabidze (1895–1937) exposed the high costs to Georgian literature of the literary elite's decision to side with the tsar

[50] I use "imperial sublime," which functions in the context of this article as the antithesis of the anticolonial vernacular, in the influential sense outlined by Harsha Ram in his study of Russian Romantic poetry, *The Imperial Sublime*. For another endeavor to consider the relation between the imperial sublime and anticolonial vernacularity in Caucasus literatures, see Rebecca Gould, "Topographies of Anticolonialism: The Ecopoetical Sublime in the Caucasus from Tolstoy to Mamakaev," *Comparative Literature Studies* 50.1 (2013): 87–107.

[51] Bakhtin, "Slovo v romane," 84.

against the north Caucasus mountaineers. Georgian intellectuals' divided consciousness in this regard has been
a major topic in modern European Kartvelogy (Georgia
Studies).[52]

In the context of the cultural split that bisected the
Georgian intelligentsia, the admiration expressed by the
Grigol Orbeliani, the Georgian poet who participated in
the Russian conquest of Daghestan, for Qazbegi's first
major work, *Elguja* (1881), marks a turning point in
Georgian literary history. In the margins of his copy of
Droeba, the newspaper in which *Elguja* was serialized two
years before his death, Orbeliani inscribed: "Amazing! I
am overjoyed. [Qazbegi] is the Georgian Homer." Referring to Qazbegi by his penname, "Troublemaker"
(Mochxubaridze), Orbeliani proclaimed: "May God
bless you, Mochxubaridze, for the joy this story has
given to my heart."[53] Although there is no gainsaying the
rifts between an intelligentsia that facilitated colonization, and an intelligentsia that, like Qazbegi, countered

[52] See Manning, "Describing dialect," 22; Valerie Le Galchier-
Baron, "L'invention de la montagne en Georgie: le 'realisme romantique' d'Aleksandre Q'azbegi," *Revue des Études Géorgiennes et Caucasiennes* 8–9 (1992–1993): 151–175; and Oliver Reisner, *Die Schule der
georgischen Nation. Eine sozialhistorische Untersuchung der nationalen
Bewegung in Georgien am Beispiel der 'Gesellschaft zur Verbreitung der Lese-
und Schreibkunde unter den Georgiern'* (Wiesbaden: Reichert Verlag,
2004).

[53] Orbeliani's words in this and the preceding sentence are taken
from Beso Zhghenti, "Aleksandr Kazbegi," in Aleksander Kazbegi,
Izbrannye proizvedeniia, trans. F. Tvaltvadze and A. Kocheova (Tbilisi:
Zariia Vostoka, 1955), 11. Zhghenti unfortunately does not indicate
his source for this quotation.

the imperial sublime with an anticolonial prosaic vernacular, Qazbegi's conjoining of literature and ethnography brought these constituencies, however briefly, together.

For centuries, Georgian authors have played a double
role in befriending Muslim mountaineers while suc-
cumbing to the lures of empire. Orbeliani recognized
and admired this duality in Qazbegi's depiction of the
challenges faced by *Elguja*'s female protagonist, the Circassian Mzagho. In a typical Qazbegian plot that pits
Georgian aggressors against innocent Muslim mountaineers, Mzagho is kidnapped by the Georgian officer Givi,
who has been corrupted through his association with
the Russian colonizers, and forced to become his wife
against her will. Orbeliani perceived in Qazbegi's depiction of Mzagho's suffering a critique of the imperial
army in which he had served as a high-ranking officer
while conquering Daghestani lands. The alliance between cosmopolitan poetics and imperial conquest in
Georgian literary history necessitated the radical break
with the past pioneered by Qazbegi's anticolonial vernacular prosaics.[54]

As meticulously as with any Dutch painting that has
shaped European understandings of vernacularity, Qazbegi's anticolonial vernacular methodologically depicts
everyday life among the mountaineers.[55] Although his

[54] For this alliance, see Ram, *The Imperial Sublime*, and Ram and
Shatirishvili, "Romantic Topography."

[55] For the link between Dutch realism and the aesthetics of
modern prose, see Rebecca Gould, *"Adam Bede*'s Dutch Realism

early fiction partakes of melodrama, Qazbegi's later anticolonial vernacular prosaics is saturated with the everyday. This prosaic aesthetic is on display in the opening of "Eliso" (1882), published the same year as *The Parricide*, and translated in this volume. "Eliso" narrates the deportation of Chechens to Ottoman lands in drastically prosaic terms. "Fires kindled inside the circle," the narrator writes, "boiling the common meal for the night. Women prepared food, while old men sat on logs, smoking their tobacco pipes silently."[56] Unless they had not just learned in the preceding sentence that "a group of carts crammed with furniture stood in a circle, guarded by Russian troops," readers would have no reason to suspect that the Chechens are facing imminent catastrophe.

Qazbegi understood the forced migrations that the colonial regime inflicted on Chechens and other mountaineers as catastrophes of nonepic proportions. He also discerned in this distance from the epic register the danger that, because it does not lend itself to poetry, the Chechen experience would never be given literary form, and thus would never be rendered, and never be known, to the outside world. To paraphrase Morson, what art represents it misrepresents, and what it does not represent goes unrepresented. When readers are conditioned by a literary culture that recognizes only the imperial sublime as worthy of attention, they are less attuned to

and the Novelist's Point of View," *Philosophy and Literature* 36.2 (2013): 423–442.

[56] Aleksandre Qazbegi, "Eliso," in *Txzulebata*, 1: 385.

vernacular literary form. This aesthetic education leaves them unequipped to deal with the everyday disasters of colonial rule, and powerless to address the conundrum famously underscored in Marx's dictum "They cannot represent themselves, they must be represented."[57] Colonialism's crisis of representation is also a crisis of literary form. Due to its inability to register how the banality of colonial governance affects everyday life, a poetics premised on the imperial sublime cannot adequately account for the experience of colonialism among the colonized.

By way of overcoming readers' natural imperviousness to others' mundane suffering, Qazbegi's prosaics reminds the reader of that "unrealized surplus of humanness" that is a precondition for empathy, in life as in art. It cultivates an aesthetics of empathy that cannot easily be given poetic form, and which risks being dismissed as "sentimental." Although Qazbegi's writings have been dismissed on the grounds of excessive sentimentalism by later scholars and critics, his emphasis on empathy—which is neither wholly realist nor Romantic—might better be understood as one dimension of his anticolonial prosaics.[58] With respect to the prosaic evocation of affect, Qazbegi's aesthetics aligns with that

[57] This was famously cited as the epigraph to Edward Said's *Orientalism* (New York: Vintage, 1978). Said's citation is from Marx's *The Eighteenth Brumaire of Louis Bonaparte* (1852).

[58] For an influential attempt to recover this (largely female gendered) aesthetics for North American literature, see Nina Baym, *Woman's Fiction: A Guide to Novels by and about Women in America, 1820–1870* (Ithaca: Cornell University Press, 1978).

of the Russian novelists such as Dostoevsky, who inspired Bakhtin and who have also been dismissed by later writers as overladen with sentiment.[59]

When, in Tolstoy's *War and Peace*, Prince Andrei tells Pierre that the outcome of battles is determined by "a hundred million diverse chances which will be decided on the instant by whether we run or they run, whether that man or this man is killed," he elaborates a prosaic aesthetic, which however is neither vernacular nor anticolonial.[60] Equally evocative of the aesthetic imperative for art to represent life in its rawness is the assertion of Dostoevsky's protagonist in *A Raw Youth* that the novelist "possessed of a longing for the present [*toskoi po tekushemu*]" and unsatisfied by the historiographic mode of narration that stresses closure at the expense of possibility and structure at the expense of chaos, must be willing to "guess and make mistakes" when he undertakes to represent the world around him.[61] Qazbegi took seri-

---

[59] I refer primarily to Nabokov's influential reading of Dostoevsky, for which see his *Lectures on Russian Literature*, ed. Fredson Bowers (New York: Harcourt Brace Jovanovich, 1981), 110.

[60] Leo Tolstoy, *War and Peace*, trans. Ann Dunnigan (New York: Signet, 1968), 930. Cited in Gary Saul Morson, "Contingency and Freedom, Prosaics and Process," *New Literary History* 29.4 (1998): 676.

[61] Fyodor Dostoevskii, *Podrostok*, in *Polnoe sobranie sochinenii F.M. Dostoevskago* (St. Petersburg: Tip. P.F. Pantelieeva, 1904–1906), 9: 529. Interestingly, the passage in which this comment occurs has been interpreted as Dostoevsky's indirect critique of the literary method of *War and Peace*, precisely for Tolstoy's subordination of art to "historical form" and his refusal to confront the messiness of reality in his prose. For this line of argument, see Morson, *The Boundaries of Genre*, 12.

ously the prosaic insight that reality is governed more by sentiment and passion than by the well-regulated laws of poetic form.

The Parricide's protagonists Nunu and Iago are among Qazbegi's most memorable characters. These star-crossed lovers are prevented from joining their lives together by the power imbalance between serfs and the class of Georgians who serve in the tsar's army, and who are known by titles such as *diambeg* and *esaul*. In terms of the anticolonial vernacular, Nunu and Iago's tragedy is even more affecting than the broader paradoxes of colonial rule that serves as its ultimate cause. While, for Dostoevsky, a writer in whose literary spirit he fashioned his works, the dialectic of faith and doubt is the central axis around which human experience turns, for Qazbegi, politically induced suffering is the key tension. In keeping with Bakhtin's understanding of novelistic discourse as a system that incorporates multiple social registers and genres, and which, while heterogeneous when viewed externally, attains coherence from within, Qazbegi's anticolonial vernacular is most successful when it portrays individual political disenfranchisement as the effect of systematic oppression.[62]

Notwithstanding the posthumous critical disdain for Qazbegi's aesthetic excesses, Qazbegi's importance to Georgian literary history is beyond contestation. The Soviet Georgian scholar Beso Zhghenti noted the shock *Elguja* elicited among the Georgian literary public following its publication. "*Elguja*," writes Zhghenti, "elic-

---

[62] Bakhtin, "Slovo v romane," 72.

ited general astonishment. For the first time in Georgian literature, mountaineers appeared as heroes. The resonant and deep *dramatic* images of courageous . . . mountaineer peasants fighting for their honor and freedom . . . [and] marked by integrity of character and high morals, at once found their way to the reader's heart."[63] Similarly focusing on Qazbegi's flair for the dramatic, Rayfield observes that Qazbegi invested his fellow Moxeves and their Chechens and Circassian neighbors with "universal tragic force, and brought into the epic of their folk legends the structures of Greek tragedy."[64] While both observations usefully reclaim aspects of Qazbegi's aesthetics that cannot easily be assimilated to vernacular realism, they miss the distinctiveness of Qazbegi's prosaics, which consciously replaces, in aesthetic terms, an imperial sublime with an anticolonial vernacular. Qazbegi has his share of melodrama. Even this formula, however, does not fully capture where Qazbegi's distinctiveness as an artist lies.

Qazbegi's uniqueness consists rather in what he does with the prosaic flow of time, with the "perfect, warm night, one of those evenings when a person feels blessed to be alive, when pleasure surges through every coil of every vein" that opens "Eliso."[65] As Morson phrases it, such narrative gestures awaken us to "events that we do not appreciate simply because they are so common-

[63] Zhghenti, "Aleksandr Kazbegi," 11, emphasis added.

[64] Donald Rayfield, *The Literature of Georgia: A History* (Oxford: Clarendon Press, 1994), 198.

[65] Qazbegi, "Eliso," 385.

place."[66] These events are prosaic in that "a small but real measure of choice exists at every instant," and in the way their unfolding makes available different kinds of pasts, and implicitly, different possible futures.[67] Most genres and literary discourses are temporally flexible, but prosaics, as articulated and refined by Bakhtin and Morson, is uniquely able to conjure, represent, and hence to generate, the unstructured flow of time.

Notwithstanding the formally innovative aspects of Qazbegian anticolonial vernacular prosaics, it is the ethical dimension of Qazbegi's aesthetic that earns him a permanent position in the history of anticolonial literature.[68] Qazbegi's depictions of the lives of Chechen mountaineers remains unsurpassed, even among other thematically related achievements in the realm of prosaics, including Tolstoy's better known chronicle of the mountaineer encounter with colonialism, *Hadji Murad* (1912). "Eliso" chronicles the forced banishment of the Chechens and other Muslim mountaineer communities from the Caucasus to the Ottoman Empire that followed the tsarist conquests of the 1860s and 1870s. In keeping with Bakhtin's concept of novelistic discourse as one that is constituted through the interrelations of heterogeneous genres, Qazbegi's "Elberd" draws on ac-

[66] Morson, "Prosaics: An Approach to the Humanities," *American Scholar* 57.4 (1988): 519.

[67] Morson, "Contingency and Freedom, Prosaics and Process," 683.

[68] This line of Qazbegi criticism was pioneered by the Georgian literary critic Kita Abashidze (1870–1917). See his *Etiudebi XIX saukunis kartuli literaturis istoriidan* (Tbilisi: Sabchota Sakartvelo, 1962), 353–438.

tual newspaper clippings and reconstructed dialogues to narrate the story of a Chechen man sentenced to death by hanging for trying, unsuccessfully, to prevent a Russian soldier from raping his wife. But, as the next section argues, Qazbegi's most extended engagement with Chechen thematics occurs in *The Parricide*.

Qazbegi's Chechens

Qazbegi wrote about Chechens in terms that prior Georgian authors had restricted to Georgian mountaineers. Many authors have aimed to represent their cultural others persuasively, but few have done so successfully. Stories such as "Eliso" richly attest to Qazbegi's investment in the specificities of Chechen culture, which anticipate the comparably ethnographic incorporation of Avar, Chechen, and Qumyq lexicons into the text of Tolstoy's *Hadji Murad*.[69] In keeping with the anticolonial vernacular's mandate to evoke ethnographic life worlds in terms of their own experience, Qazbegi similarly intersperses his narrative with Chechen phrases such as *marsho dooghiil* ("Come in freedom"—a standard Chechen greeting).[70]

Bakhtin described this prosaic form of ventriloquism well when he stipulated that, in contrast to the poet, the

[69] For Tolstoy's use of indigenous Daghestani sources, see Uzdiat Bashirovna Dalgat, *L.N. Tolstoi i Dagestan* (Makhachkala: Dagestanskoe knizhnoe izd-vo, 1960).

[70] Qazbegi, "Eliso," 395; tk of this volume.

prose writer partakes in the "unfolding of social heteroglossia [*sotsialnoe raznorechie*] surrounding the object,
the Tower of Babel mixture of languages that circulate
around any object, [and] the dialectics of the object . . .
interwoven with the social dialogue surrounding it."[71]
While the incorporation of foreign languages is only one
element in the prosaist's repertoire, it does distinguish
the short story writers, novelists and ethnographers who
chronicled the Caucasus from their poetic counterparts,
including Pushkin, Grigol Orbeliani and Aleksandre
Chavchavadze, whose sublimely imperial aesthetics prevented them from cultivating the anticolonial vernacular.

As noted above, Qazbegi's ethnographic fictions are
contemporaneous with the first published ethnographies
of the northern Caucasus by Chechens and Ingush authors. The *Compendium of Research on the Caucasus Mountaineers (Sbornik svedenii o kavkazskikh gortsakh)*, published
in Tbilisi in ten volumes from 1868 to 1881, was the
primary venue for the publication of such ethnographies
in Russian. These Russian publications were paralleled
by an emergent ethnographic tradition in Georgian,
which was however still in its infancy at the time of
Qazbegi's writing.[72] The frontispiece for the journal's

[71] Bakhtin, "Slovo v romane," 92.

[72] Such works include Mate Albutashvili's, *Pankisis xeoba: istoriul-
etnograpiuli da geograpiuli aghtsera* (1898), ed. G. and N. Javaxishvili
(Tbilisi: Kartul kavkaziuri urtiertobis tsentri, 2005), and, for the
Soviet period, the writings of Sergi Makalatia, Tedo Saxokia, Giorgi
Tedoradze, Besarion Nizharadze, Giorgi Chitaia, Alexi Ochiauri,
and Natela Baliauri. See the discussion of the latter two ethnographers in Paul Manning, "Love Khevsur Style: The romance of the

ninth volume (figure 3) encapsulates well the aesthetic that shaped the readerly tastes of its editors and contributors. This opening image mixes a nineteenth-century predilection for generic embellishment—witness the Darial Gorge encapsulated in a flower frame—with a vernacular embrace of local rhythms of time and place. The waters of the Darial, where Eliso's beloved Vazhia was killed, lap below, amidst a cavalcade of mountaineers and their ubiquitous carts ascending the peaks. Similarly evocative, although harkening back more to the imperial sublime, is the striking depiction of this same gorge, dated 1862, by the Russian landscape painter Ivan Aivazovsky (1817–1900; figure 5). Stirred by the many different aesthetic currents on display in such images, Qazbegi looked beyond the mountain landscape that had already formed the bedrock of the Georgian and Russian imperial sublime. More innovatively, and arguably for the first time, his prosaics also engaged with the mountains' inhabitants.

In the hands of ethnographers such as Laudaev and Akhriev, Caucasus ethnographies drew on a panoply of prosaic devices to give their subjects verbal flesh. Qazbegi also composed non-fictional ethnography, with serialized essays such as "Moxevians and their Life," which ran in *Droeba* over the course of 1880.[73] In con-

mountains and mountaineer romance in Georgian ethnography," in *Caucasus Paradigms: Anthropologies, Histories, and the Making of a World Area*, eds. Bruce Grant & Lale Yalçın-Heckmann (Münster: LIT Verlag, 2006), 23–46.

[73] Aleksandre Qazbegi [published under the name A. Mochxubaridze], "Moxeveebi da imati tsxovreba," *Droeba* (1880): 156–167.

tradistinction to other contemporaneous Russian and Georgian ethnographies, which treat the mountaineers as "ethnographically separate from states and historical life," Qazbegi narrates "the ethnographic life (*qopa*, *tsxovreba*)" of the mountaineers as one that is shaped by "exchanges with the Russian state and its local Georgian comprador class [to which Qazbegi belongs], that is, by an endless series of imposts, fines, impressments into forced labor, and most of all, bribes to avoid all of these."[74]

Qazbegi's ethnographic aesthetics situates his protagonists squarely within contemporary political life. He combines a deep immersion in local life ways with an embrace of prosaics. In Bakhtin's account, urban prosaists turned in earlier eras to "street songs, proverbs [*pogovorki*], [and] anecdotes" as they carried out a "lively play with the 'languages' of poets, scholars, monks, knights and others" in their literary experiments.[75] Far removed from the urban milieu, ethnographic prosaists like Qazbegi, Laudaev, Akhriev, and Dalgat engaged with local customs, indigenous languages, and religious rituals and processions, as they collectively created a prosaic vernacular that, even when not always explicitly anticolonial, consistently differed from the normative aesthetics of the imperial sublime. Their writing codified a new literary medium for the indigenous communities newly included within the colonial fold. In literary terms,

[74] Paul Manning, unpublished draft of *Semiotics of Drink and Drinking* (London: Bloomsbury, 2012).
[75] Bakhtin, "Slovo v romane," 86.

these writers furthered the vernacularization of Caucasus literatures, and heralded its break with the imperial sublime that dominated Georgian literary culture a generation earlier.

In *The Parricide*, Qazbegi introduces Imam Shamil—the Avar military leader whose Islamic state Orbeliani helped to dismantle, and in whose army Anzor Cherbizh of "Eliso" had served—to his readers as Chechen. The historical Shamil was in fact Daghestani. Qazbegi's slip reveals the symbolic capital that Chechens possessed for the author and his readers. Chechens for Qazbegi operate within a society more equitable and just than the socially stratified if more "civilized" plains. "Chechens never knew slavery [*batonqmoba*]," writes Qazbegi in a typical ethnographic aside, because "they considered each other equal."[76] After refashioning Shamil as Chechen, Qazbegi establishes a lineage for his hero leading from the mountains to the plains. Shamil, we are told, wanted to "unite his people, heart and soul, to the Georgians."[77] As a prototype of mountaineer resistance, Shamil was refashioned by Qazbegi as a freedom fighter who sought alliances with Georgians. Qazbegi's framing set the terms of many later Georgian reflections on Shamil's legacy, most significantly by the major twentieth-century novelist Mixeil Javaxishvili (b. 1880), who was executed in 1937 for his divergence from Stalinist aesthetics. Javaxishvili's novelistic account of another famous figure in the history of Caucasus anticolonialism,

---

[76] Aleksandre Qazbegi, "Mamis mkleveli," in *Txzulebata*, 1: 303.

[77] Qazbegi, "Mamis mkleveli," 303.

the Georgian *abragi* (social bandit) Arsena Odzelashvili, is clearly inspired by Qazbegi's precedent.[78] As Rayfield rightly notes, both novels address "the discontent of the Georgian peasantry not just with their own feudal masters, but with Russian rule and with the Russian officers who with brutal beatings, deportations and hangings, enforced that rule," and both do with an eye to elaborating an anticolonial vernacular in prose.[79]

One strategy adopted by Qazbegi for representing Chechens to a non-Chechen readership was to render them as Christian. This act of cross-confessional domestication suggests that certain types of local affiliations penetrated more deeply than religion for Qazbegi. In terms of Tuite's distinction between the anti-ethnographic and pseudo-ethnographic in Georgian literary history, Qazbegi's impulse to domestic his Muslim characters by denominating them Christian fulfills antiethnography's allegorical mandate, which uses foreign characters to elucidate local realities. At the same time, *The Parricide* is a pseudo-ethnography, inasmuch as it is set in Georgia, in familiar surroundings. All that is unfamiliar about the text are its Chechen protagonists.

Although Qazbegi's framing was anachronistic, it was based on a substratum of historical actuality, for,

[78] For the most recent edition of this heavily redacted and many-times censored text, see Mixeil Javaxishvili, *Arsena Marabdeli: romani*, ed. Nana Suxitashvili (Tbilisi: Sakartvelos Matsne, 2005).

[79] Donald Rayfield, "Time Bombs: the Posthumous and post-Soviet reinterpretation of two Georgian Novels," in *Art, Intellect and Politics: A Diachronic Perspective*, eds. G.M.A. Margagliotta and A.A. Robiglio (Leiden: Brill, 2013), 584.

as many ethnographers have documented, pagan traditions persisted among the Caucasus mountaineers well
into the modern era.[80] This pseudo-ethnographic domestication of a foreign, if neighboring, people is evi-
dent when the Chechen hero of *The Parricide*, Parcho,
proposes to his fellow Georgians as they hide in the
mountains and prepare to raid the plains below that
they "go worship at the cross." Predictably, the Georgian Christian mountaineer Koba agrees to Parcho's
plan enthusiastically. More surprising is that the initiative to pray in Christian fashion is taken by a Muslim
Chechen. Parcho's initiative to pray as a Christian re-
flects Qazbegi's pseudo-ethnographic eagerness to represent Georgia's cultural others as variations on Georgian selves. In Qazbegi, the anticolonial vernacular becomes an ethical commitment to recognizing the other
pseudo-ethnographically. This results in a literary mode
that Bakhtin would later famously theorize as novelistic
discourse.

Together with much of Daghestan, medieval Chechnya was included within the Christian empire ruled over
by the Georgian Queen Tamar (r. 1184–1213). One of
the most commonly cited proofs of Georgia's influence
during this period is Txaba-Erde, a Christian church dat-
ing back to the eleventh-century, and located in present

[80] For a comprehensive overview of the pagan practices of the
north Caucasus, see the monographs of Mariel Tsaroieva, *Anciennes
croyances des Ingouches et des Tchétchènes: peuples du Caucase du nord* (Paris:
Maisonneuve et Larose, 2005); *Peuples et religions du Caucase du Nord*
(Paris: Karthala, 2011); and *Tusholi: la dernière déesse-mère du Caucase*
(Paris: Éditions du Cygne, 2011).

day Ingushetia, on the border with Georgia. Georgian
scholars have documented tablets found in the church
that are inscribed with words in the Vainakh (Chechen–Ingush) language using the Georgian alphabet.[81]
This small piece of evidence for the historical depth of
the cultural exchanges between Chechens and Georgians
could be multiplied by further examples from Daghestan.[82] Qazbegi's representation of Parcho's willingness
to utter Christian prayers builds on popular Georgian
traditions, while imparting to them a new political, and
anticolonial, edge. In keeping with Qazbegi's wish to
eradicate religious difference, Parcho and his Georgian
comrades make a pact on the site of a church after Parcho's call to Christian prayer had already conjoined Chechen and Georgian belief systems into an allegorical
unity that is anti-ethnographic (in Tuite's sense, an in-
version of the ethnographic rather than its negation)
because it is premised on the erasure of cultural difference.

Islam became normative in Chechen belief systems
only in the eighteenth century. Its influence was uneven,
and often difficult to distinguish from popular pre-
Islamic beliefs, even following the Islamicization of

[81] See D. Gunia, "Satadzro reliepiuri figuruli gamosaxule-
bebi–mati roli da mxatvruli xasiati kavkasiis xurotmodzghvarul
skolata kontekstshi," *Proceedings of II International Congress of Caucasi-
ologists* (Tbilisi: Ivane Javaxishvili State University, 2010), 61–62,
224–225.

[82] For some sources, see Magomed Gasanov, "On Christianity
in Dagestan," *Iran & the Caucasus* 5 (2001): 79–84, and P. K. Uslar,
"Nachalo khristianstva v Zakavkazie i na Kavkaze," *SSKG* 1 (1869).

Chechnya.[83] Until that period, Chechen and Ingush religious beliefs partook almost exclusively of pan-Caucasian paganism, with an admixture of Christianity. Many Chechens and Ingush today fondly recall Christian elements in their cultural pasts, even as they rigorously follow Islamic rituals.[84] Qazbegi's portrayal of his Chechen protagonist in terms that argue for family resemblance to his Georgian counterparts testifies to the author's desire to project a composite Georgian–Vainakh culture onto an ethnographic present. What was at stake for Qazbegi in blurring religious, linguistic, and cultural boundaries between Georgians and Vainakh peoples? Qazbegi sought alternatives to urban literary traditions. He wished to critique Georgia's "comprador" colonialism in prose. Inventing Chechen heroes enabled Qazbegi to confront his Georgian readers with an anticolonial vernacular vision of a mountaineer polity untainted by the cowardice of the plains.

Afterlives of an Oeuvre

My fieldwork in Tbilisi, which began in 2014 and continues into the present, has brought me into contact with many Georgians who dwell on the shame that Qazbegi's idealiza-

---

[83] For the history of Islam in Chechnya, see Anna Zelkina, "Islam and Society in Chechnia: From the Late Eighteenth to the Mid-nineteenth Century," *Journal of Islamic Studies* 7.2 (1996): 240–264.

[84] For further delineations of these syncretic paradoxes, see Rebecca Gould, "Secularism and Belief in Georgia's Pankisi Gorge," *Journal of Islamic Studies* 22.3 (2011): 339–373.

tion of Imam Shamil and other anticolonial warriors induced in them. One interlocutor spoke of how Qazbegi's rage was directed against his fellow Georgians, including so she felt, herself, who had failed to live up to Shamil's courageous standards. "It is as though Qazbegi hates his fellow Georgians for betraying ourselves," this undergraduate at Tbilisi State University said. Qazbegi was Georgia's first modern novelist to incorporate mountaineers on both sides of the Caucasus, north and south, into a common cultural geography. His anticolonial prosaics interrogates the historical constitution of Georgian self-identity while also placing colonial ambitions, including the aesthetics of the imperial sublime, under critical scrutiny.

Qazbegi was also, in Manning's words, "the only true Georgian *narodnik* [populist]," who forsook his family's tradition of service to the ruling regime and instead chose to become a shepherd.[85] The French travellers in the first story translated in this collection, "Memoirs of a Shepherd," mocked Qazbegi precisely on these grounds. Qazbegi chose his life, like his prosaics, deliberately, in the belief that prose alone could sustain the ethical vision he pursued across narratives of forced deportation, parricide, and colonial conquest. Unlike his Romantic predecessors who cultivated the imperial sublime in verse, Qazbegi saw his anticolonial aesthetic as most conducive to prose.

Qazbegian prosaics rejects the poetry of conquest in favor of the prose of critique. Without wishing to suggest that prose is intrinsically more adept at resisting violence, or more politically engaged than poetry, it is worth asking

[85] Paul Manning, *Strangers*, 65.

why Qazbegi preferred prose to poetry at this particular historical juncture. Equally, it is worth interrogating the relation between vernacularity and anticolonialism, which may be regarded as a key diacritic of modernity on colonial borderlands. As Manning points out, the years intervening between "the publication of Chavchavadze's letters [of a Traveller] (1861–1871) and Aleksandre Qazbegi's first writings about the Moxevians (1880)" were marked by "the development and consolidation of a specifically Georgian print culture. . . . in the newspaper *Droeba*."[86] While *Droeba's* Tbilisi location caused the newspaper to be inflected by the rhythms of urban life more than by the grandeur of the mountains, the discussions that took place in this newspaper set the stage for more comprehensive engagements with colonial legacies in subsequent generations. Most notable among Qazbegi's progeny is Mixeil Javaxishvili whose historical fiction, in particular the much-censored *Arsena Marabdeli* (composed 1925–32; published 1933–36), develops Qazbegi's anticolonial theme, and who paid an even higher price than did Qazbegi for his opposition to the dominant politics of his time.[87]

[86] Manning, *Strangers*, 78.

[87] For an excellent discussion of the many levels of censorship to which *Arsena Marabdeli* was subjected, see Donald Rayfield, "Time Bombs," 584–589. For a similarly anticolonial orientation in a Soviet poet who was executed the same year as Javaxishvili, see Titsian Tabidze, *Rcheuli natsarmoebi*, eds. I. Abashidze, R. Gargiani, and D. Sturua (Tbilisi: literatura da xelovneba, 1966), especially his poem "Gunib" 1: 106 (discussed in detail in Rebecca Gould, *The Literatures of Anticolonial Insurgency* [New Haven: Yale University Press, 2016], chap. 3).

Taken as a whole, Qazbegi's work carves out a place for affect in the anticolonial aesthetic, and it evokes readerly empathy with mountaineers whose lives lack the glamour of the classical heroes of the sublime epics. These mountaineers include such figures as Elberd and Eliso's father Anzor Cherbizh. For Qazbegian prosaics, as for prosaics generally, the smaller and more inconsequential a character, the more obscure, marginalized, and oppressed a person is, the more profound is his or her significance. Like Father Zosima in *The Brothers Karamazov*, Qazbegi's narrators insist on the importance of minor acts performed, for good or for evil, every day. "You pass by a small child," says Zosima to his auditors, "you may not have noticed the child, but he has seen you." This exchange of glances, both conscious and unconscious, is thereby inscribed onto the child's "frail heart" for the remainder of his life.[88]

Qazbegi's anticolonial vernacular cultivates an aesthetic that Orbeliani's generation ignored, even though, as we have seen, these earlier poets could also be moved by Qazbegi's prose. Like Thoreau, who organized a much briefer excursion into nature when he moved to Walden Pond, Qazbegi prized the autonomy of the unshackled imagination above all else, in literature as in life.[89] By relentlessly subjecting imperialism—including

[88] Fyodor Dostoevskii, *Polnoe sobranie sochinenii* (St. Petersburg: Prosveshchenie, 1911–1918), 16: 60.

[89] For the timeline of Thoreau's stay of his stay by Walden Pond (1846–1847) as well as his writing process, see Richard Lebeaux, *Thoreau's Seasons* (Amherst: University of Massachusetts Press, 1984), 210–211.

its promulgation through poetic form—to prosaic inter-
rogation, Qazbegi became the greatest regional prosaist
Georgian literature has ever known. Future scholarship
on his work, hopefully in a comparative context attentive to parallel ecocritical interventions in other geographies, will make it possible to understand his contribu-
tion to the global critique of colonialism.

This essay has tracked the convergence of vernacularity and anticolonialism in the oeuvre of a writer
whose imagination traversed multiple moments in the
colonial encounter. Morson and Emerson's argument
that what is missing from "formalist and narratological
approaches to the novel" is a "prosaics of prose," works
also as a critique of existing Qazbegi scholarship, which
is astonishingly sparse for languages other than Georgian.[90] Qazbegi continues to be read with reference to a
poetics rather than a prosaics, as if, under the conditions
of colonialism, a text can only attain to the condition of
literature by in some way reconciling itself to a sublime
aesthetics that severs art from life.[91] While Bakhtin dedi-

[90] Gary Saul Morson and Caryl Emerson, *Mikhail Bakhtin: Creation of a Prosaics* (Stanford: Stanford University Press, 2000), 19.

[91] One example of Qazbegi scholarship that focuses on poetics
at the expense of prosaics includes Sergo Manasevich Dzhorbe-
nadze, Vano Shaduri and Valerian Itonishvili, eds., *Aleksandre Qazbegis biograpiisa da shemokmedebis sakitxebi* (Tbilisi: Tbilisis universitetis
gamomcemloba, 1987). Two of the eight essays in this collection
(pp. 111–133 and 151–173) examine Qazbegi's "poetics [*poetika*]"
while none consider what may have been specific to his prose. In
fairness, it should be noted that Bakhtin's book on Dostoevsky,
originally entitled *Problems in Dostoyevsky's Art* (*Problemy tvorchestvo*

cated much of his life to dislodging the prejudical privileging of verse over prose, the implications of this intervention for anticolonial vernacular prosaics remains largely unprobed.

The aesthetic and ethical implications of prosaics reach well beyond Qazbegi's oeuvre. One perspective that has been missing so far from explorations into the potential of prosaics to elucidate the contours of everyday life is how this aesthetic works in colonial contexts. While Bakhtin primarily conceptualized prosaics as a way of coming to know neighbors who speak our languages but in different registers, the colonial situation presents a more heteroglossically attenuated context that is ineradicably marked by imbalances of power underwritten by colonial law. Chechens who spoke Russian, the language of their colonial masters, frequently considered themselves, or sought to become, members of the colonizing class. And yet these Russophone intellectuals, among whom should be included Laudaev, Akhriev, and Dalgat, also inaugurated ethnographic writing within their respective cultures, albeit in Russian.

In contradistinction to the utopian strands in Bakhtinian dialogism, heteroglossia under the conditions of colonial rule often facilitated dominance instead of bridging social difference.[92] In such contexts, heteroglossia

Dostoevskogo, 1929), appeared in a second edition, revised by the author, as *Problems in Dostoevsky's Poetics* (*Problemy poetiki Dostoevskogo*, 1963).

[92] For the relation between the science of linguistics and colonial rule, see Joseph Errington, *Linguistics in a Colonial World: A Story of Language, Meaning, and Power* (New York: Wiley, 2010).

indexed the linguistic gaps that underwrote norms of colonial governance. Qazbegian prosaics pursued a path different from that pursued by the archetypal polyphonic novelist, Dostoevsky, for whom the rise of popular journalism served much the same function as ethnography did for Qazbegi. Dostoevsky's characters come to know each other in spaces of geopolitical if not absolute neutrality. Even when their actions are fraught with imbalances of power, this power is not inflected by the cultural and religion differences that are constitutive of colonial governmentality. In Dostoevsky, nearly everyone is Christian, and those who are not Russian are simply excluded from the dialogic situation. By contrast, Qazbegi's protagonists are preemptively interpolated into uneven distributions of power. Frequently, there is no way for them to escape from the force field fostered by these political arrangements. Given its many historical divergences from more familiar norms, the task of interpreting and extending Qazbegian anticolonial vernacular prosaics is a project for a postcolonial future. This volume has aimed to contribute to such an agenda.

Appendix: Qazbegi in Translation

Standard Georgian edition:

Txzulebata sruli krebuli (Tbilisi: sabchota mcerali, 1948) (Four volumes). This is the edition I have used for this translation.

Russian (in chronological order):

Ottseubiitsa. Trans. V Gol'tsev (Moscow: Gos. izd-vo khudozh. lit-ry, 1936).

Povesti. Trans. A. Neiman (Tbilisi: Zaria vostoka, 1936).

Aleksandr Kazbegi: izbrannoe. Trans. Yelena Gogoberidze (Moscow: Khudozhestvennoi literatura, 1949).

Izbrannoe. F. Tvaltvadze, A. Kochetkova (Tbilisi: Merani, 1974).

Turkish:

Elguca ile Mzago. Trans. Ahmet Özkan Melasvili (Istanbul: Sinan Yayinlari, 1973).

Chechen:

Hairzinars: Davinarg; Cicija; Elisa. Trans. Iu. Morgashvili (Grozny: Noxkh-Ghalghayn Izd-vo, 1961). This translation has been anthologized in V. A. Dykhaev: *Nokhchiin sovetski literatura* (Grozny: Nokhch-Ghalghain knizhni izd-vo, 1978), 116–126.

Czech:

Translation of "Xevisberi Gocha" in *Kamenité cesty Gruzie (Povídky gruzínských klasiku)* (Prague: SNKLHU, 1958).

Lithuanian:

Darjala krauja: romani un novels. Trans. Margarita Niedre (Riga: Liesma, 1977).

French:

By the famous Indo-European linguist Georges Dumezil: translations of "Xevisberi Gocha," "Elguja," and *Mamis mkevleli*, respectively as "Goca, le chef de vallee," "Elguja," and *La Parricide*, published posthumously in *Revue des Études Géorgiennes et Caucasiennes* 5 (1989), 6–7 (1990–1991), and 8–9 (1992–1993).

Le confesseur (Liège: Solédi, 1930).

German:

Eliso. Trans. Steffi Chotiwari-Jünger (Herzogenrath Shaker 2014). Includes Translations of "Cicia," "Eliso," "Xevisberi Gocha."

Film Versions:

Eliso, Dir. Nikoloz Shengelaya; written by Nikoloz Shengelaya and Sergei Tretyakov (Tbilisi: 1928), 70 min. Silent film with Russian subtitles.

Recommended Secondary Scholarship:

Benasvili, Dimitri. *Aleksandre Qazbegi* (Tbilisi: Sahelgami, 1939). One of the earliest biographies of Qazbegi, in Georgian.

Gozalisvili, Salva. *Alek`sandre Qazbegis xelnacerebi: agceriloba* (Tbilisi: Sakartvelos MAG, 1960). Description of Qazbegi's unpublished manuscripts.

Gould, Rebecca. *The Literatures of Anticolonial Insurgency* (New Haven: Yale University Press, 2016).

—. "Aleksandre Qazbegi's Mountaineer Prosaics: The Anticolonial Vernacular on Georgian-Chechen Borderlands," *Ab Imperio: Studies of New Imperial History in the Post-Soviet Space* 15.1 (2014): 361–390. The afterword to this book is a revised version of this article.

—. "Topographies of Anticolonialism: The Ecopoetical Sublime in the Caucasus from Tolstoy to Mamakaev," *Comparative Literature Studies* 50.1 (2013): 87–107.

—. "Secularism and Belief in Georgia's Pankisi Gorge," *Journal of Islamic Studies* 22.3 (2011): 339–373.

Le Galchier-Baron, Valerie. "L'invention de la montagne en Georgie: le 'realisme romantique' d'Aleksandre Q'azbegi," *Revue des Études Géorgiennes et Caucasiennes* 8–9 (1992–1993): 151–175.

Manning, Paul. "Describing Dialect and Defining Civilization in an Early Georgian Nationalist Manifesto: Ilia Ch'avch'avadze's 'Letters of a Traveler,'" *Russian Review* 63.1 (2004): 26–47.

—. *Strangers in a Strange Land: Occidentalist Publics and Orientalist Geographies in Nineteenth-Century Georgian Imaginaries* (Brighton: Academic Studies Press, 2012).

Milton Keynes UK
Ingram Content Group UK Ltd.
UKHW011435180624
444387UK00033B/614

9 786155 053528